Deemed 'the father of the scientifi[c]
Austin Freeman had a long and dist[inguished career as]
a writer of detective fiction. He was born in London, the son of a
tailor who went on to train as a pharmacist. After graduating as a
surgeon at the Middlesex Hospital Medical College, Freeman
taught for a while and joined the colonial service, offering his skills
as an assistant surgeon along the Gold Coast of Africa. He became
embroiled in a diplomatic mission when a British expeditionary
party was sent to investigate the activities of the French. Through
his tact and formidable intelligence, a massacre was narrowly
avoided. His future was assured in the colonial service. However,
after becoming ill with blackwater fever, Freeman was sent back to
England to recover and, finding his finances precarious, embarked
on a career as acting physician in Holloway Prison. In desperation,
he turned to writing and went on to dominate the world of
British detective fiction, taking pride in testing different criminal
techniques. So keen were his powers as a writer that part of one of
his best novels was written in a bomb shelter.

THE SURPRISING EXPERIENCES OF MR SHUTTLEBURY COBB

R Austin Freeman

HOUSE OF
STRATUS

This edition published in 2001 by House of Stratus, an imprint of Stratus Holdings plc, 24c Old Burlington Street, London, W1X 1RL, UK.

www.houseofstratus.com

Typeset, printed and bound by House of Stratus.

A catalogue record for this book is available from the British Library.

ISBN 0-7551-0380-7

CONTENTS

CHAPTER ONE

The Gifted Stranger

The humblest of creatures play their useful, and sometimes indispensable, parts in the great scheme of Nature. My introduction to the strange events connected with the Gifted Stranger was effected by a mere railway guard, and a mighty unceremonious one at that. He had blown his ridiculous whistle and waved his absurd flag, the engine had uttered a warning shriek, and the train had actually begun to move, when I raced wildly up the platform at Herne Hill.

"'Ere, in you get!" shouted the guard, spitting out his whistle and wrenching open a door; and, as I scrambled on the footboard, he applied a *vis a tergo* that sent me staggering across the compartment and caused the only other occupant hastily to draw up his foot and rub that portion of his boot that corresponds to the corn on the little toe.

"Seem to be in a hurry," the proprietor of the toe remarked sourly.

"I'm not really," I replied. "It was the guard. I am sorry I trod on your foot."

"So am I," was the acid rejoinder. And the conversation languished.

I put my bag and stick in the rack and spread myself out. It was a first-class compartment, my ticket was a third, and the first stoppage was at Faversham. This was highly gratifying. We all like to get some of our own back from the railway companies.

My companion sat and stared out at the house roofs that floated past the window as if immersed in his own reflections. He was a massively-built man with large feet, a sandy moustache, and a peculiarly foxy type of countenance. Socially I could not place him at all. He did not look like a professional man, or a farmer, or a ship-master, or, for the matter of that, like a first-class passenger. But that was none of my business.

Presently he produced a letter from his pocket, and, holding it nearly at arm's length, slowly read it through. Now I object strongly to people who read letters under your very nose, for, try as you will, you can't help an occasional glance, and then you are annoyed with yourself. This was a long letter, written in a bold, legible hand on both sides of the paper and held out in the full light of the window. I tried to look away, but again and again my eyes unconsciously turned towards it and each time I found myself reading a sentence before I recollected myself. What made it worse was that the sentences were so very odd that they tempted me to steal a further glance to see what they meant, and my struggles to resist the temptation were not so successful as I should have wished.

"If it is really true, there is a fortune waiting for somebody."

I had read this sentence before I had the presence of mind to shut my eyes. And even while I was considering the question, If what was true? behold! my eyes had automatically opened and taken in another sentence.

"Your peculiar gifts and experience ought to help you to solve it."

I turned my eyes away guiltily, but could not help speculating. What were his peculiar gifts – besides a hypersensitive little toe? And what would they help him to solve? Before I was aware of it, my eyes were back on the paper and had lighted on this astonishing statement:

"It is in the room in which there is an iron pump and a sedan chair."

Good Heavens! I ejaculated inwardly. What kind of room can it be that contains an iron pump and a sedan chair? And what can the rest of the furniture be like? In my amazement I stared at the letter like a fool, and at that moment I caught the eye of the owner.

It was very embarrassing. Of course I oughtn't to have looked at the letter, but then he ought not to have held it under my nose. And, in any case, it was rude of him to stare at me as he put the letter away and then to move pointedly to the other end of the compartment. I felt it very much and for some time sat gaping out of the window in great confusion, trying to ignore my fellow passenger.

When, at length, I ventured to glance in his direction, I again caught his eye. But now there was a new expression in it; an expression of interest and lively curiosity. He held a number of official-looking blue papers in his hand, and, when he caught my glance, he hastily gathered them together — so hastily that he dropped one, and before he could snatch it up from the floor, I was able to observe that it had a photograph pasted on it. He seemed unreasonably annoyed about the accident — for it was only a man's portrait, after all. He rammed the papers into his inside breast pocket, buttoned his coat, stuck his hands deep into his pockets and looked as if he would have liked to stick his feet in, too, and so generally put himself out of sight. For the rest of the journey he sat motionless in his corner, staring out of the window like a cataleptic waxwork, evidently determined to offer no further entertainment.

But he had given me some food for reflection to go on with. There was the room, for instance, which contained a pump, a sedan chair and "It." What on earth could "It" be? A stuffed elephant, perhaps, or a full-size model of the *Victory*, or some similar portable trifle. And then my companion's "peculiar gifts and experience", what could that mean? Was he a clairvoyant or a crystal-gazer? He didn't look like one. But there was that photograph, and here my thoughts wandered off into speculative channels, which led nowhere, as I had not his peculiar gifts.

From these wanderings I presently came back to my own affairs. I had been sent down to Canterbury by old Morlett, our senior partner, on business connected with a property called Elham Manor. The rather ruinous old house had been taken by an American gentleman, Mr Jezreel P Damper, for one year on trial, with the understanding that, if he liked it, he should take it on lease. He had already been given possession but had apparently not entered into residence, and my business was to inspect the premises and make local arrangements for the execution of such repairs as I thought necessary, consulting with Mr Damper if he was to be found. When I had done this I was to take a fortnight's holiday.

At Canterbury West my gifted fellow-traveller alighted and walked slowly towards the barrier. I bustled past him, and, unostentatiously presenting my third-class ticket, hurried out of the station, down the approach into the High Street. Jubilantly I took my way along the venerable thoroughfare towards the massive towers of the West Gate, anxiously considering where I should put up for the night, until my eye lighted on the jovial sign of the Falstaff Inn. Now a real painted sign is in these days a thing to be thankful for, and such a painted sign, too, to say nothing of the fine forged ironwork. I halted to admire the portrait of jolly Sir John, then, on the front of the house, I descried the winged wheel of the CTC, whereupon I dived in through the low doorway and demanded high tea and a night's lodging.

There is great comfort in an old-fashioned inn with a painted signboard and a landlord who knows what's what. I sat complacently in the coffee room and watched a minor canon, disguised as a waiter, prepare the table for afternoon service and vanish silently. I sniffed a growing aroma of grilled ham, and when, anon, the canon reappeared, staggering majestically with a Falstaffian tea tray, I drew up to the table, poured myself out a bumper of tea, and decapitated a soft-boiled egg at a single stroke. And at that very moment the coffee-room door opened and in walked my peculiarly gifted fellow-traveller.

He did not appear to notice me, which was uncomfortable. I am not a conspicuous man, but I am quite visible to the naked eye at a distance of seven feet, which was the distance that separated us as he sat at the other end of the table pretending that I didn't exist. It was not only uncomfortable, it was offensive. Perhaps his toe still rankled in his breast – if I may use the expression – or my inadvertent glance at his letter was still unforgiven. In any case his glum and silent presence at the table destroyed all pleasure in my meal. It was neither solitude nor company. Hurriedly I gobbled up eggs, ham and toast, drained the teapot to the last drop, rose from the table and stalked out of the room.

A couple of minutes later I was once more strolling up the High Street, debating whether I should begin my business at once or wait till the morrow. Entering the city by the West Gate, I paused on the bridge to look down on the quiet river, the flock of resting boats, and the picturesque houses with their thresholds awash, leaning over their unsteady reflections, when, chancing to look back, to my surprise and annoyance I observed the gifted stranger sauntering towards me.

It was very singular. I had left the inn only a few minutes and when I came away he had but just begun his meal. This indecorous haste in feeding further prejudiced me against him, which, together with a dim suspicion that he was following me, made me decide to get clear of him. Starting forward, I strode down a by-street, darted through an archway and along an alley and then traversing a narrow lane once more found myself in the High Street.

A careful look round showed me that the gifted one was not in sight. Probably he had gone down the by-street and missed the archway. I was turning to resume my walk when I perceived straight before me the entrance of the City Museum. Now museums have a fascination for me, especially provincial museums, which are apt to contain antiquities of local interest. The present one, too, offered a sanctuary from my gifted acquaintance, for if he was really following me, he would probably spend the rest of the day scouring the streets in search of me. Accordingly I entered the museum and began to browse round the galleries, of which the first two that I entered were tenanted by a dreary company of stuffed birds. From the ornithological rooms I passed to a picture gallery furnished abundantly with examples of the old masters of the "brown and shiny" school. This was not very thrilling. What was more to the point was a notice on the wall directing visitors to the Coplin Collection of local antiquities. Following the direction of the pointing hand, I started forthwith along a narrow passage that led to a distant annexe, which, to judge by its present condition, was seldom trodden by the foot of man. At the end of the passage I came to a large room, at the threshold of which I halted with a gasp of recognition. For the first thing that met my eye was a sedan chair, and the second, a curious iron pump.

This, then, was the mysterious room. The next question was What was "It"? I ran my eye over the various objects displayed confidingly on tables, unguarded by glass covers. "Leather corset, said to have been worn by Queen Elizabeth," and extremely contracted in the region of the gizzard. That wasn't it. "Ivory recorder with silver key." That wasn't it. "Wheel-lock musket," "Child's Shoe," "Carved horn drinking-cup," none of these fitted the implied description. And, at last, I came to the veritable "It".

No doubt was possible. I identified it at the first glance. Mystery and secrecy exhaled from it like a subtle perfume. Concentrating my attention to a perfect focus, I bent over the table to examine it minutely.

It was a silver mirror, a small piece, of charming design and exquisite workmanship, wrought – mirror and frame together – from a single plate of silver. The few square inches of polished surface were surrounded by a broad, richly ornamented frame, the design of which included an encompassing ribbon which supported an oblong pendant. And here was where the mystery came in. For on ribbon and pendant was engraved, in delightfully picturesque "old face" lettering, the following strange inscription:

"A Harp and a Cross and goode redd golde,
Beneath ye Cross with ye Harp full nigh,
Ankores three atte ye foote of a tree
And a Maid from ye Sea on high.
Take itt. Tis thine. Others have stepped over.
Simon Glynn. 1683."

I read through this poetic gem a half a dozen times and was none the wiser then. In sporting parlance, it was a "fair knockout". I could make nothing of it. At length I turned to the descriptive label for enlightenment – and didn't get it.

"Small silver mirror, discovered in 1734, concealed in an aumbry in Elham Manor House. This house was built by Simon Glynn, a goldsmith and an official of the mint under the Commonwealth, who lived in it for many years. The aumbry was discovered behind the panelling of the dining room during some repairs. The mirror is believed to be Glynn's own work and the doggerel verses engraved on the frame are supposed to refer to some hidden treasure, but their exact meaning has never been ascertained. See Boteler's 'Manor Houses of Kent', for an account of Simon Glynn and Elham Manor House."

Here was news indeed! Elham Manor! I had the keys in my pocket at the very moment! And I had full authority to carry out any structural repairs that I thought necessary! And the cryptogram had never been deciphered!

Now I understood that mysterious sentence in my friend's letter: "There is a fortune waiting for somebody." Yes, indeed! Perhaps it was waiting for me. I seemed to understand, too, why the gifted one had dogged me in that singular manner. No doubt his letter had contained some helpful tips and he suspected that I had read them – and I wished I had, now. But he little suspected that I had the run of Elham Manor, and I mustn't let him if I could help it.

Feverishly I copied into my notebook the inscription and the label. Then I wandered round the room, thinking hard and looking at the exhibits. Should I repair to the adjoining library and look up Boteler, or should I make a beeline for the Manor House? I turned over this question before the pump, the shoe, the pistol and the recorder, but could not make up my mind. I cogitated as I stood in front of the sedan chair, vainly seeking to peer in through the curtained windows. In sheer absence of mind, I tried the fastening, and when, to my surprise, the door came open, revealing the snugly-cushioned interior, I became suddenly possessed by an insane curiosity to feel what the inside of a sedan chair was like. Yielding to the impulse, I backed in and sat down, and then, to complete the sensation, I drew the door to, when it shut with an audible click.

I sat in the semi-darkness turning over my problem. Should I risk the publicity of the reading room or go direct to the Manor House? And what the deuce could Simon Glynn mean by that absurd doggerel? The sedan chair was extremely comfortable, and the dim light that filtered in through the worn curtains was pleasant and conducive to thought. I enjoyed myself amazingly – until my ear caught the sound of approaching footsteps and an unmistakable clerical voice. Then, thinking that it was high time to move, I gave a gentle push at the door.

But the confounded thing wouldn't budge. I pushed a little harder, but the door only creaked protestingly. It evidently had a snap catch. In short, I was locked in. I was about to try if the front window could be let down when the footsteps entered the room and a sonorous clerical voice arose in wordy exposition. I broke out into a cold perspiration and hardly dared to breathe – especially as the dusty interior was inducing a distinct tendency to sneeze.

"Here is a sedan chair," the voice expounded, "a vehicle which illustrates – leave that handle alone, James, you are not allowed to touch – which illustrates the primitive modes of locomotion in use among our forefathers. You will observe – "

Here I seized my nose with both hands. My eyes watered. My shoulders heaved. I tried to hold my breath, but it was no go. I felt it coming – coming – and at last it came.

"*Ha chow!*"

The expounding voice ceased. There was a deathly silence. And then, in stern accents:

"How many more times am I to remind you, Alfred, of the indecorousness of sneezing in public places?"

"Please, sir, it wasn't me," piped a small, protesting voice.

" 'It wasn't *me*'! You mean, I presume, 'It was not *I*.' And don't make your bad manners and bad grammar worse by prevarication. I heard you. Let us move on."

They moved on. The solemn exposition continued. And then they moved off. As their footsteps retreated, I made a tentative attack on the front window, but hardly had I grasped the webbing strap when my ear caught a faint creak. There was someone in the room, still, a person with one slightly creaky boot. I heard the creak travel slowly round the room, halting at intervals. Then it made a prolonged halt – in the neighbourhood of the mirror, as I judged by the sound. And meanwhile I sat and perspired with anxiety.

Presently the creaking boot moved on again. It travelled more quickly now; and it began to travel in my direction. Slowly, gradually it approached, nearer and nearer it came, until, at last, it was opposite my prison. And there it paused. I held my breath until I was like to burst. How much longer was the idiot going to stand there staring like a fool at an ordinary, commonplace sedan chair?

I was on the very verge of suffocation when something touched the handle. Then it turned slowly; the door opened, and there − yes − my prophetic soul! it was − my highly gifted friend. He looked in at me with sour surprise and hastily closed his note book. But he made no remark. After a prolonged stare he made an attempt to shut the door, but I had the presence of mind to stick my foot out. Then he turned away. I listened to his footsteps retreating down the passage at a slow saunter until they were faint in the distance, when their rhythm suddenly changed to that of a quick walk. He was off somewhere in a great hurry − probably to the library to consult Boteler.

I stepped out of my prison with my mind made up. I would go and make a preliminary inspection of Elham Manor and read up Boteler when I had seen it. Striding briskly down the passage and through the galleries I came out into the street and turned towards the road to Sturry. I knew my way, for I had looked it up on the Ordnance Map. The old house stood on a side road between Sturry and the village of Bouldersby, only a mile or two out of the town.

It was a pleasant summer evening and the sun was still shining brightly as I came out on the country road and took my way blithely past farm and meadow and tree-shaded oast. About a mile and a half from the city I came upon a finger-post inscribed "Bouldersby and Hawkham", and pointing up a byroad bordered by lofty elms. Taking this direction I walked on for another mile or so until a bend in the road brought me suddenly to what I recognised at once as my destination, a low, red-brick wall abutting on the road and above it the stepped gables and lichen-covered roof of an ancient and highly picturesque house.

I walked along in front of the wall until I reached the iron gates, and here I halted to reconnoitre. For that ridiculous jingle of old Simon Glynn's rang in my head anew as I looked at the front of the old house. The iron gates were hung from two massive brick pillars, each surmounted by a stone pineapple, and on the front of one pillar was carved in high relief a shield bearing a St George's cross, while the other bore a relief of a shield with an Irish harp.

Here, then, were the Harp and Cross plain enough, but the other items mentioned in the doggerel were not so obvious. It is true that, between the windows above the porch, was a carved brick niche containing a statue of a young woman, and a very charming little statue it was, evidently the portrait of a young Puritan lady; but whether she came from the sea or the land there was nothing to show. There was, however, a good deal to show what interpretation had been put on the doggerel rhyme, for the flagged path from the gate to the porch seemed to have suffered from a succession of earthquakes. And the excavators had not stopped at the path; the pillar that bore the Cross device was sensibly out of the perpendicular, showing that its very foundations had been rooted up, and the brickwork itself showed numerous patches where treasure-seekers had bored into it. Evidently the gifted one and I were by no means the first explorers in this field.

I had just taken the keys from my pocket, and was selecting the one that belonged to the gate, when the silence was broken by a faint rhythmical sound from the road round the bend. It was the creak of a boot — one boot, not a pair — and as I listened, it seemed to me that I had heard it before. I slipped the keys back into my pocket — for it would be better not to be seen entering the house — and was beginning to saunter up the road, when the creak materialized into my gifted competitor, coming round the bend like a lamplighter. He slowed down suddenly when he saw me, and as I strolled round another turn in the road, I observed that he had stopped and was gazing about him with his back to the house, as if he had not noticed it.

I walked on towards Bouldersby considering the situation. My respected rival was evidently nervous and suspicious of me. He thought I knew a good deal more than I did. And this suggested the question: How much did he know? Apparently that letter had contained some useful information which he suspected me of having extracted. But if it was true that the treasure was still undiscovered, and he had some private information that I had not, perhaps it would be as well to keep an eye on him and see if I could pick up a hint or two from his proceedings.

I had just reached this sage conclusion and was on the point of turning back, when I perceived, a little way ahead, a small roadside inn; a picturesque little house, standing back from the road behind a small green, on which was a signpost bearing the sign of the Royal George. The pleasant aspect of the house led me to approach and reconnoitre when I observed that it had a back wing extending into a garden and that the garden ran down to the river and adjoined an orchard. I approached past the little bay window (in which was a card inscribed with the legend "New-laid Eggs") and looked in at the door. It was a most primitive inn. A couple of barrels on stands and a row of mugs on a shelf formed its entire outfit, and the only persons visible were an old woman, who sat sewing busily in a Wycombe armchair, and a corpulent tabby cat.

The homely comfort of the place, the quiet and the proximity of the river, offered an agreeable suggestion. As the old lady looked up and smiled a greeting, I advanced and ventured to enquire:

"Do you happen to have any accommodation for a lodger?"

Mine hostess nodded and smiled as she replied: "Yes, they're all new-laid. I keeps my own fowls and feeds 'em myself."

This seemed irrelevant. Raising my voice considerably, I asked:

"Could you put me up here for a week or so?"

"Oh, apples!" she answered doubtfully. "No, they're hardly ripe yet. It's a bit early, you see."

The reply was a little disconcerting. But its dogged as does it. I tried again. With an ear-splitting yell that was like to have swept the mugs off the shelf, I repeated my question – and was asked in return whether I would have mild or bitter?

It seemed hopeless. But I liked the look of the place. It was scrupulously clean and well kept; and the rustic quiet, the pleasant garden and the river flowing past, urged me to new efforts. I scribbled my question on a scrap of paper which I handed to the old lady; but observing that this seemed to give offence, I hastily added a line explaining that I was suffering from a sore throat and had lost my voice. This completely appeased her and she allowed me to continue the negotiations on paper, of which the upshot was that, if I was content to "live plain and not expect too much waiting on", I could have the small bedroom overlooking the garden and move in to-morrow evening.

I walked back towards Elham Manor in high spirits. I had secured pleasant country lodgings and a convenient base from which to carry out the repairs and explorations on the old house and keep a watch on my rival. That was a good start, and now I would make a preliminary inspection of the house – if I could do so unobserved – and then look up Boteler's history.

When I came in sight of the Manor House, my rival was nowhere to be seen. But I approached warily in case he had climbed over into the grounds to begin his explorations, and I had a good look round before inserting my key into the gate. As I turned the key, I noted the excellent condition of the lock – which seemed to have been recently oiled – and the same thing struck me when I unlocked and opened the front door. Apparently our tenant, Mr Damper, had begun his restorations with an oil can.

I walked with echoing footsteps through the hall and into the empty rooms, wondering dimly how I should communicate with Mr Damper, but thinking more of Simon Glynn and his hidden treasure. The fine old house was falling slowly but surely into decay. Such repairs as would make it really habitable would leave no corner of it undisturbed and must surely bring to light the secret hiding place if it really existed. Thus reflecting, I wandered from room to room, noting the dilapidations and speculating as to the whereabouts of the treasure, until I came to a chamber at the end of the building which was at a slightly lower level. Descending the short flight of stairs, I tried the massive door, and, finding it locked, produced the bunch of labelled keys. As I inserted the first key, I thought I detected a faint sound of movement from within, and the unpleasant idea of rats suggested itself, but I worked away until I found a key – labelled "Butler's Pantry" – that turned in the lock. The heavy door swung open with a loud creak, and I entered the room, which was in almost total darkness, the only source of light being a few chinks in the shutters.

Dark as it was, however, there was light enough for me to see a very strange and unexpected object, to wit, a small but massive chest which stood on the bumpy oaken floor near to one window. I drew near to examine it, and then found that it was fastened only by a bolt, though it was clearly intended to be secured with a padlock. In mere idle curiosity, I drew back the bolt and raised the lid, and then I got a mighty surprise. For even in that dim light it was easy to see that the contents were of no ordinary value. Rings, pendants, bracelets, brooches, glittered and sparkled in the dim light; gold chains were heaped together like samples of cable in a ship-chandler's, and the interstices of the pile were filled in with a litter of unmounted stones.

I was positively staggered. What made it still more astonishing was that this was obviously not Simon Glynn's treasure. The chest was a new one and the jewels were not only fresh and bright but were manifestly modern in character. That I could see at a glance. But what this treasure was, how it came here, and to whom it belonged, were questions to which I could suggest no answer.

I knelt down by the chest and began to turn over the articles one by one. I am no great judge of jewellery, but it was evident that some of these things were of very great value. Here was a pendant, for instance, of which the central diamond was half an inch in diameter. That alone must be worth some hundreds of pounds. I picked it up to look at it more closely – and at that instant both my wrists were seized in a vice-like grip. I dropped the pendant and, uttering a yell of surprise, began to struggle to free myself. But the grip only tightened; gradually my hands were forced together on my chest; something cold touched my wrists; there was a metallic click, and, glancing down, my astonished gaze lighted on a pair of handcuffs.

"Now, it's no use kicking up a dust," said a voice close to my ear. "I've got the cuffs on you, so you'd better come along quiet."

I twisted my head round to get a view of the speaker, and succeeded in catching a glimpse of half a face. But that was enough. It was – my prophetic soul again – the gifted investigator. And one of his peculiar gifts I was now able to sample – a most uncommon degree of muscular strength.

"I've got you, you know," he resumed unpleasantly. "You can't get away, so you'd better chuck up the sponge and come quietly."

This was all very well, but I am not a naturally submissive person. I made no comment, but, straightening myself suddenly like a mechanical jumping frog, I capsized him backwards and began to make play with my legs. It was an undignified affair, I must admit. We rolled over and over on the floor; we pummelled and prodded one another ambiguously and without purpose, and once I cut short an eloquent remonstrance by planting my knee in the middle of his abdomen. But the odds were against me, and the end of it was that I reclined on my back with his knee on my chest and listened to the terms of surrender.

But now a most astonishing thing befell. Even as he leaned over me and expounded the folly of my conduct, I was aware of a dim shape behind him, noiselessly approaching. A face – a foreign-looking face, with a waxed moustache and fiercely-cocked eyebrows – appeared over his shoulder and slowly drew nearer and nearer. I gazed with fascination, and the words of wisdom trickled unheeded into my ears; and still the face drew nearer. Then came a sudden movement, a shout of surprise from the gifted one, another shout, and a sound of sixteen heavy portmanteaux falling down a steep flight of stairs.

Released from the weight of my assailant, I sat up and watched events. My eyes, accustomed by now to the dim light, took in a heap of squirming humanity from which issued a stream of breathless objurgation. I counted six legs – all in violent movement – and reasonably assumed the existence of three individuals. One pair of legs, incomparably the most active, I identified speculatively, by the stockinged feet, as those of my late assailant, for he must have removed his creaky boots to have approached me so silently, which now placed him at a disadvantage, as the other two warriors wore their boots – and used them.

Presently, from the writhing mass, a man partially detached himself and began to angle for the wildly-kicking feet with a loop of cord. For some time he was unsuccessful and the feet had the best of it – unless his head was unusually hard – but at last the loop slipped over the ankles and was drawn tight; on which the gifted one made appropriate comments in terms unsuitable for verbatim report and ending in a muffled snort. The loop having been secured by one or two round turns and a knot, the two strangers rose, breathing heavily and rubbing certain apparently painful spots on their persons. Meanwhile, my late adversary lay motionless and silent, his legs lashed together and his wrists secured by handcuffs; and now I understood that curious snort that had cut short the flow of his eloquence, for I observed that my rescuers had tied a gag over his mouth.

I ventured, at this juncture, to draw attention to my own condition. But it was unnecessary. The two strangers approached me, still rubbing themselves. I held out my manacled hands to have the gyves unlocked, when, to my astonishment, one of the foreign rascals pushed me down and sat on my stomach while the other took a few turns with a cord round my ankles. I protested vigorously.

"Here! I say! You're making a mist – " I didn't get any further, for one of the foreign brutes dabbed something into my mouth and tied it there with a string behind my neck. Then he issued a command to the other miscreant in some ridiculous jargon which I suppose served them in place of a language, and the other villain hurried out of the room. He returned in less than a minute and made some report in his wretched substitute for speech, and the two wretches then picked up my unfortunate and gifted acquaintance and carried him away.

I lay on the floor reflecting, with profound misgivings, on my alarming situation. Evidently I and my rival had unwittingly discovered the hiding place of a gang of thieves, and those scoundrels were going to put us out of the way of doing them any mischief. That was clear. But what was our destination? Were they going to drop us in the river? Or would they convey us to some cellar or vault and knock us on the head? Either possibility was equally likely and equally unpleasant.

My meditations were cut short by the reappearance of the two miscreants, who, without a word, picked me up by my arms and ankles and marched away with me. Up the stairs, into the hall and out through this on to the flagged path, we went, like a somewhat hurried and premature rustic funeral; and we were just approaching the front gates when another very singular thing happened. I was being borne head first, while my captors marched facing forward, and I was thus able to command a view of the rear. Now, as we approached the gate, chancing to turn my eyes towards the flanking wall that separated the garden from the orchard, to my unutterable surprise I saw three heads slowly rise from behind it. Each head was, naturally, furnished with a face, and each face was adorned with one of the very broadest grins that I have ever seen. It was really a most astonishing affair.

Outside the gates a closed fly was drawn up, otherwise not a creature was in sight. The door was opened by the driver and I was bundled in and deposited on the back seat, the other half of which was occupied by my gifted friend, whose boots had been considerably placed on his knees. The two ruffians entered and shut the door, the driver mounted to his seat, and away we went at a smart trot.

I was relieved to note that we were not being driven towards the river, and was rather surprised to find that our route lay towards the town. But it was not merely towards the town; it soon became evident that the town itself was our objective. The audacity of these villains was positively staggering! Heedless of the risk of detection, these miscreants bore us, manacled, bound and gagged, not merely through the outlying suburbs, but into the very city. Jostling cabs, carts, vans and carriages, past the teeming footways and busy shops, we passed unblushingly into the High Street itself, and then, turning down a well-frequented side street, came at length to a halt. I directed my astonished eyes out of the near window, hardly able to believe in such brazen audacity; and the first object they encountered was a blue glass lamp bearing the inscription "Police Station".

The driver sprang down and opened the door, the two "foreign devils" hooked me out of the seat and carried me swiftly in through the open doorway to a large office, where they deposited me on the floor and hurried away without a word. A police inspector and a sergeant looked in amazement from me to the departing ruffians and then looked at one another.

"Rum go, this," said the inspector, with another doubtful glance at me. "I hope it's all right, but they'd no authority to make arrests."

Here the two ruffians returned, bearing my unfortunate companion, at the sight of whom the inspector's face assumed a distinctly careworn expression.

"I seem to know this man," he said in a low voice. Then, addressing our captors, he asked: "Who are these two prisoners?"

"Zey are two of ze gang," the senior ruffian replied carelessly; "I do not know vich two. I find zem quarrelling about ze booty. I catch zem. Zey are here. Enough," and he began superciliously to roll a cigarette.

"Take off the gags, sergeant," said the inspector, and as he spoke he, himself, untied mine and pulled me up into a sitting position, while the sergeant did the same for my fellow-sufferer.

"Now," said the inspector, addressing the latter, "what's your name?"

"My name, sir," replied the gifted one with as majestic an air as is possible to a man who is seated on the floor with his feet tied together, "is Burbler, Detective-Sergeant Burbler of the Criminal Investigation Department."

"Hanged if I didn't think so," murmured the inspector. "Take off the cuffs, sergeant, and untie his feet. You've made a mistake, gentlemen. You've arrested one of our officers."

"I sink not," the foreign person replied haughtily. "Zat man is a criminal. Look at 'is face. I haf experience;" and he calmly lighted his cigarette.

"You'll have some more experience when I get these handcuffs off," said Burbler; but here the inspector interposed, forbidding violence and demanding explanations.

"How did this affair happen?" he asked.

"I'll tell you," Burbler replied, savagely. "I was sent down here to look out for this Chicago-St Petersburg gang. From information received I was going to Elham Manor where I expected to find traces of them, when I met this man Polopsky" (here he actually pointed to me!). "I recognised him at once from his photograph – I've got it here," and he pulled out from his pocket the photograph which I had seen in the train, and showed it to the inspector, who examined it closely, and, having remarked that it "seemed rather a poor likeness", returned it. "Well," pursued Burbler, "I followed him and saw him hanging about Elham Manor, and, when he saw me and sneaked away, I got into the house by a back window and waited. Presently he came back and let himself in with a key and went to a locked room and entered that with another key. I followed him in and caught him with a lot of the stolen property in his possession, a whole trunk-load of it."

"Where is the stolen property now?" the inspector asked.

"I suppose it's in the house still," replied Burbler, and he continued furiously: "Well, I had just overpowered Polopsky and got the cuffs on him, and was about to secure the property, when these two blithering lunatics rushed in, and – well, you see what happened. I'm going to prosecute them for assault and unlawful arrest."

"Better not," said the inspector. "Russian Secret Police, you know. Exceeded their powers, of course, but better not make a fuss. You are going to charge Polopsky, I suppose?"

Burbler grunted assent, and turning to me said:

"Louis Polopsky, I arrest you on the charge of burglary and forgery, and I caution you that anything you may say will be used in evidence against you. Do you want to make any statement?"

"I should like to remark," I replied, "that my name is not Polopsky; and that, if any damage is done to the premises of Elham Manor through your coming away and leaving the door and gates unlocked, I shall hold you responsible."

The inspector looked at me suspiciously and asked: "What do you say your name is?"

"My name," I replied, "is Shuttlebury Cobb, of the Firm of Morlett and Griller, solicitors to the landlord of Elham Manor, and I am, at present, in charge of the property."

I handed the inspector some papers and a draft agreement that I had in my pocket, together with a bunch of labelled keys; and while he looked them over, the rather chap-fallen detective put on his boots.

"It seems to me," I continued, "that you have all been making rather free with our premises. May I ask if those other three men were some of your people?"

"What other three men?" the inspector asked in a rather startled tone.

"The men who were watching us as we left the house."

"*What men?*" demanded the inspector, the two foreign devils and Sergeant Burbler in a frantic chorus.

"The men who were in the orchard, watching us over the wall."

Burbler sprang to his feet, with one boot unlaced. For one moment the four officers and the station sergeant stared at me in silence; for another moment they stared at one another; then, with one accord, they made a rush for the door.

I followed them out. The fly was still waiting at the kerb, and the five men were endeavouring to enter it simultaneously by the same doorway. I watched their frantic struggles. I saw them finally pack themselves in; and, when the inspector had snorted out the destination, I saw the fly drive off. Then I slowly wended my way back to the Falstaff and bespoke a substantial dinner.

CHAPTER TWO

The Secret Code and the Castaway

Up to that eventful day on which my firm sent me down to Canterbury on business connected with the tenancy of Elham Manor, the even tenor of my life had been uninterrupted by any cataclysms or abnormal occurrences. But from the moment in which I set forth on that apparently prosaic errand, I seemed to be taken into the charge of some exuberantly sportive jinn. The whole world appeared to go mad with one accord. I became the plaything of erratic chance, the football of circumstance; and circumstance seemed to have a decided leaning towards the Rugby game…

After the explanation at the police station, I naturally thought I had heard the last of that absurd business.

But I hadn't.

Our tenant not having arrived yet, I had a good deal of time on my hands, for I could not begin the repairs in the house until I had seen him; and the fact that I had found Detective-Sergeant Burbler still prowling about the premises induced me to keep clear of the place for the present and devote myself to a study of the surrounding country.

One of my earliest jaunts was along the road that leaves the city towards the north; a pleasant, sylvan road though somewhat trying as to the gradients.

"Wot ye not wher ther stont a litel toun,
Which that icleped is Bob-up-and-doun

Under the Ble, in Canterbury way?"

That was the road only that I passed Harbledown on my left hand and "bobbed up and down" through Blean and across the hills beyond until I finally bobbed down past Bostal mill to the seashore at Whitstable.

It was a delightful walk – with one exception. There happened to be another man going the same way. That is the worst of country roads. In a city street the passing multitudes leave one solitary and undisturbed, but on a quiet country road, a single foot passenger, going in the same direction, destroys the solitude completely. Naturally he walks at about your own pace. If you try to outwalk him or lag behind, he occupies your attention; if you try to ignore him, his obtrusive figure ahead or his irritating footfall from behind break in continually on your meditations. My present companion wore spectacles and looked like a German. Not that I would reproach him on that account. I don't suppose he wore spectacles by choice, and, of course, the poor creature couldn't help being a German. I merely record the facts.

At the top of Bostal Hill he halted to survey the Harbour down below through a pair of prism binoculars, and I took the opportunity to nip on ahead and rid myself of him.

It was in an oyster shop near Whitstable Harbour that the plot began to thicken. In spite of a substantial tea at the Falstaff, the sight of dainty and delicate natives peeping coyly from barrels at the shop door, acted as a lodestone to draw me into the little parlour, where already a couple of gourmets were seated before a gargantuan dish, regardless of the interested observers who peered in through the window. I ordered a dozen "royals", and, taking a seat at an empty table, entertained myself with the conversation of the other two customers, pending the arrival of my own meal.

"And you really think I might venture, doctor?" said one of them, a dyspeptic, nervous-looking young man, casting a look of gluttonous alarm at the dish.

The jovial faced medicus peppered an oyster with deliberate care.

"Well," said he, "it's your own affair, you know. Chances about a million to one against enteric in these beds. Still, I shouldn't eat too many" – there were two dozen on the dish. "Of course, at my age the risk is infinitesimal, but at yours – well, you must use your own judgment," and here the doctor diminished his own chance of immunity by one millionth and smacked his lips.

Nearly ten minutes elapsed. I had just poured myself out a glass of stout as a preliminary to the feast, the doctor had swallowed his sixteenth oyster with an audible "gollop", and his companion was apprehensively munching his last slice of brown bread and butter, when there lurched into the room a large man of seafaring aspect, wearing a sealskin cap. He ordered half a dozen oysters – "Quick, if you please" – and seated himself at my table, apologizing civilly with a slight foreign accent, for finishing his cigarette.

"Zome English people opject to smoke at mealtimes," he remarked.

I assured him that I had no objection whatever, on which he thanked me and began to converse affably, informing me that he was the master of a timber ship from Riga, that he was going to sea that very night, and that he would be glad to be clear of the approaches to the Thames.

"Ach! But it is a bad river, zis London river. Shoals and sandts, sandts and shoals everyvere. Noding but sandts and shoals."

As he mentioned the detested shoals, he shook his head and glared at me reproachfully, as if I had put them there, so that I felt almost constrained to apologize for their presence, and might actually have done so had not the stream of conversation been interrupted by the entry of the proprietor with a small dish.

"Not very peckish this evening, Captain Popoff," he remarked as he set the dish before his customer.

"No," replied the captain; "my appetide is spoil. Zis night I leave Englandt. Perhaps I come not again, and zen I see my goodt friendts again never."

His methods of dealing with oysters were summary in the extreme. The succulent natives might have been some sort of unsavoury medicament to judge by the way in which he disposed of them. One after another they vanished from their shells, unseasoned and unsavoured, even as grains of barley are spirited into the gizzard of a hungry fowl. In a couple of minutes the dish was cleared, and the captain, having swigged off his glass of stout, heaved a sigh of relief and drew from his pocket a gaily-coloured packet of cigarettes.

"Vill you take one?" he asked, holding the packet towards me. "Zey are very choice. You do not buy cigarettes like zese in Englandt."

It was no empty boast. The cigarette that I lighted was quite the best that I had ever smoked and I hastened to tell him so.

"Zen," said he with a gratified smile, "you will allow me to present you the packet. I have plenty more. No? Zen, perhaps, if you are not occupied you vill come and see my ship, and I vill give you a box of cigarettes for a keepsake and you shall drink a glass of vodka with me in my cabin. How do you say?"

I accepted the invitation with pleasure, and accordingly, when we had paid our reckonings, the captain and I set forth together for the harbour. As we passed in through the gates I became aware of that kind of awakening among the shipping that heralds the approach of high water. The ordinary business of the day was over. The high stages from which the coal whippers take flying leaps into space at the ends of their hoisting ropes stood idle, and the grimy baskets rested on heaps of "slack" beside the sieves. Mariners, washed and unwashed, crawled up the quay-face like geckoes with no visible means of support, on their way townward, or lounged about in groups, spinning interminable yarns. The last of the oyster smacks had taken up her moorings, the whelk boats lay stranded above tidemarks on the beach outside, and everything bore an aspect of repose excepting the outgoing craft, which were all in a state of ferment, hoisting sails and hauling on warps, all agog to get out on the top of the tide.

Alongside the end of the pier and opposite a great stack of newly landed timber lay a smallish barquentine; a shabby-looking craft with rusty white sides and a green painted underbody, intended to delude the unwary into the belief that she was coppered. Most of her sails were hoisted, and two or three sailors were aloft loosing the remainder as the captain and I approached. By the name *Anna: Riga*, painted on her counter, I judged this to be our destination, and I was right.

"'Zis is my ship," said Captain Popoff. "Ve have just time for a glass and a little smoke before ze tide is full. Zen I shall vish you farewell."

He stepped down on to the rail, and, grasping a shroud, held out his hand to me and we both dropped down on deck close to the fore hatch, which was still open.

"Ve are a little untidy," said the captain, "but you vill excuse. Shall I go first?"

Rather to my surprise, he stepped to the open hatch and began to descend a fixed iron ladder. It seemed a queer way to approach the cabin, but I made no remark and cautiously let myself down after him until I stood on the shingle ballast.

"It is very dark," said he, peering into the pitchy gloom aft. "Perhaps, as you are a stranger, I had better get a light to show you ze vay."

With this, he returned up the ladder; but no sooner had he reached the deck, than someone clapped the covers on the hatch, leaving me in total darkness. I thought this rather odd, but still had no misgivings until some three or four minutes had passed without any sign of the captain's reappearing. Then, as a clatter of falling ropes and running gear from above bespoke active preparations for departure, and sundry bumps and grinding noises suggested that the vessel was actually in motion, a sudden alarm seized me. Climbing up the ladder, I tried to push up the hatch cover, and, finding that it was securely fastened above, I fell to battering on it with my fists. This, however, produced no result, excepting a very uncomfortable soreness of my knuckles, and even when I fetched up a large stone from the ballast and hammered with it for a good five minutes, my demonstrations evoked no response.

Reluctantly and with a sinking heart, I descended the ladder and sat down on the dry shingle to think over the situation. That the captain could have forgotten me was incredible; that my persistent hammering on the hatch cover had passed unnoticed was beyond belief. The only alternative was that I had been kidnapped, that I was being spirited away, though for what purpose I was unable to conceive. The whole set of circumstances was incomprehensible. Apparently I had fallen into the hands of some sort of brigands or pirates; and yet to think of this harmless old timber knacker as a pirate seemed positively grotesque. However, the one fact was indisputable. I was being carried away forcibly to some foreign port – probably Riga; unless I was to be robbed and thrown overboard on the way. And as I reached this conclusion, a barely perceptible heave of the ballast on which I sat told me that the *Anna* was clear of harbour and fairly started on her voyage.

I don't know how long I sat moping in the darkness of the *Anna's* hold. It can have been but a short time, though it seemed to me that hours had passed since I came down that fatal ladder. And as I sat there, memories of the past and speculations as to the future chased one another through my brain. I turned over the strange events of the last few days; I thought of the queer old silver mirror that I had seen in the museum at Canterbury and the quaint doggerel verses inscribed on it; I conned over the absurd jingle of which I had a copy in my pocket, and which I had dimly hoped might guide me to the discovery of Simon Glynn's treasure, hidden somewhere in the old manor house – that grand old house that I should probably never see again, And I thought of the pleasant holiday that I was to have enjoyed in the old city and the sweet country around it; and then by a swift transition, from the might-have-been I turned to the future – dark, threatening, inscrutable.

Suddenly I was aroused by a noise overhead. The hatch covers were raised, a shaft of light shot down into the hold, and the captain's head appeared in the square opening above.

"Vould you please to come up, sir?" he asked politely.

Would I not! No lamplighter ever shinned up a ladder more actively than did I, with the purple sky above and that black cavern beneath. In a trice I was on deck, gazing sternly into the rather sheepish face of Captain Popoff.

"What is the meaning of this, Captain?" I demanded.

"You vill hear now," he replied, avoiding my eye. "It is not my affair. I cannot help it. I do as I am toldt. Zat is all. Zis vay, if you please."

I followed him slowly along the deck, taking in the position of affairs as I went. The ship appeared to be crossing the estuary towards the north, for I could see over the port rail the distant Isle of Sheppey, while, directly astern, the low Kentish shore with the twin spires of Reculver loomed faint and far away in the warm evening light. The captain preceded me on to the low poop to the deck-house door, which was opposite the wheel and down a short flight of stairs. At the bottom of the stairs he halted, and, pushing open the door, invited me to enter; which I accordingly did; and got one of the biggest surprises of my life.

Seated at the small cabin table, each with a sheaf of papers before him, were three men. I recognized them all. One was the spectacled German who had dogged me on the Whitstable road. The others were the two Russian police agents who had arrested me and the detective, Burbler, at Elham Manor. It was an astonishing meeting. The German presided, with a fat, complacent smile; the two Russians sat gloomily twisting their waxed moustaches as if they intended presently to gore me with the stiff points.

"Ach!" exclaimed the German, who seemed to be a facetious ruffian, "you are zobbrised to zee us, Mr Mifflin, and you do not seem bleased. Zat is not so mit us. Ve are delighted to meet you."

I gazed at the German and his scowling accomplices with a feeling of stupefaction and began quaveringly:

"It seems to me that there is some extraordinary mistake – " when the former interrupted: "Vot again, Herr Mifflin! No, my vreindt, it is no goot. Zat cat he vill not chomp. Ve do not make mistagues. Ve are not ze English bolice."

"Would you mind telling me who you suppose I am?" said I.

"Ve do not zubbose," he replied blandly. "Ve know. You are Chacob Mifflin, *alias* Salter, *alias* Chones and zo on. Ve follow you today from Ganderbury, ve find, fortunately a Russian ship chust about to sail, and ve catch you."

"What am I supposed to have done?" I asked.

"You are a burglar, you are a forger: but zat is not our affair. You make bombs for Polopsky and ze ozers, and zat *is* our affair. Vere are zose ozer men? Are zey still in Ganderbury?"

"I am sure I don't know," I replied. "I know nothing about those men; and my name is not Mifflin."

"Ach! Bot you haf so many names. Berhaps you vorget. Ven did you last see Polopsky?"

"I've never seen him at all to my knowledge," said I. "The last time you arrested me you said *I* was Polopsky."

"Zat vos ze English bolice vot zay zat. Ve do not mistague an American for a Pole."

Here one of the Russians interrupted impatiently: "Ve vaste time talking vid zis American pig, Herr von Bommel. Let us search his pockets."

They did so, with the dexterity of professional pickpockets, but got mighty little for their pains. A pipe and tobacco pouch, a match box, a pocket-knife, a little small change – for I had, fortunately, left most of my money at the hotel – and a pocketbook formed the entire "catch"; of which the German pounced with avidity on the last item and began eagerly to turn over the leaves.

It was a nearly new book, and most of the entries consisted of rough notes relating to the proposed repairs of Elham Manor House, which, being full of abbreviations and accompanied by calculations and hastily-drawn diagrams, puzzled my Teutonic friend not a little. But suddenly his eye lighted up, he ejaculated a voluminous "Ach!" and the two Russians craned forward to look over.

"Zo Mr Mifflin," he exclaimed, impressively, "you do not know Polopsky or ze ozers, bot yet you carry in your bocket a zegred gode. Can you oxplain zis?"

He held up the pocketbook, and I could have laughed aloud – under more favourable circumstances; for he had lighted on the absurd doggerel verses that I had copied from the ancient silver mirror in the Canterbury museum.

I endeavoured to "oxplain" how I came by the "secret code", saying nothing, however, about the hidden treasure to which it was supposed to refer. But my explanation was cut short by indignant snorts from the two Russians, and the German wagged his head admonishingly.

"Vy do you tell us zis nonsense, Mifflin, my vriendt? Haf ve not seen ze house vere your gang used to meet? Ze house vot haf a cross on von gate post, a harp on ze ozer and a statue of a yung maid above ze door? Vy do you tell us zese foolish lies? It shall do you no goot. Moch better for you if you oxplain vot you mean by zis gode. Tell us now, like a zenzible man. Vot, vor instance, is 'ankores dree'? Vot does zat mean?"

"That's just what I should like to know," said I, though it didn't seem to matter much, as I was apparently bound for Siberia.

The two Russians again snorted impatiently and even the impassive German showed signs of annoyance. Beckoning to the captain, who had been waiting by the door, he said, gruffly: "Take him avay, Cabtain. He is an opstinate fool. Ve shall gonsider zese doguments and zen ve vill talk to him again."

Accordingly I was conducted out of the cabin to a place on deck just in front of the deck-house and sheltered by the projecting roof of the latter. Here the captain placed a small cask to serve as a seat, and, having furnished me with a packet of cigarettes and a box of matches, told off one of the crew to watch me and left me to my meditations. I was glad to exchange the heat of the stuffy cabin for the comparative coolness of the open air, for it was a sultry night and seemed to grow warmer as the light faded. The darkness of the short night – it was the second week in July – was fast closing in, for it was close on ten o'clock; the land had vanished, either in the gloom or the distance, and innumerable lights began to wink and twinkle over the calm sea. At one of these – a bright light on our port bow that flashed out and faded away at regular intervals – I noticed the captain staring from time to time with an anxious and worried expression, and once he shouted out some directions to the man at the wheel.

Shortly after this, the three police officers came out on deck, and, placing each a camp stool on the main hatch a few yards away from me, sat down close together conversing earnestly in low tones and poring over my notebook by the light of a small lantern. I watched them with a faint grin as I smoked the captain's cigarettes, wondering what they would make of Simon Glynn's ridiculous jingle and what they would have to say to me when they had unravelled "the code". And so the time passed. The night closed in warm and dark; a soft breeze murmured in the sails and rigging and the ship moved (at no great pace, I suspect) over the calm sea.

It was just half past ten, as I was made aware by one of the sailors who reached past me to tap out five strokes on the ship's bell which hung above my head, when there came a sudden interruption of the quiet monotony. In an instant I found myself on the deck on "all fours", the sailor who had rung the bell and the one who guarded me staggered forward and fell sprawling at full length, and the three police officers capsized as one man and scrambled up swearing as thirty. Then the captain rushed out of the deck-house bellowing like a marine bull of Bashan, the deck filled up with excited mariners who had appeared the Lord knows whence, ropes thumped on the planks, blacks and parrels squealed from aloft, canvas flapped, and a general pandemonium prevailed.

I have never seen men so deficient in self-control. The entire ship's company, including the police officers, surged up and down the deck like a herd of bullocks. They gibbered, they gesticulated, they shouted; they craned over the side – though what the deuce they expected to see there but water I can't imagine – and one, the second mate, I believe, actually burst into tears. And all because the *Anna* had taken the ground on one of those "shoals and sandts" that the captain held in such detestation.

However, there she was, immovably seated on a sand bank with a falling tide; and there she would undoubtedly remain until the returning water rose and lifted her off. Of course, if a strong breeze should spring up from the east – or anywhere else, for that matter – she would undergo a rapid conversion into driftwood; but at present the breeze was of the lightest and the sea quite calm, save for a tiny popple of wavelets.

Gradually the excitement subsided, at least to some extent. The sails were snugged down, the sidelights taken in and an anchor light hoisted, which activities seemed to relieve the emotional tension. But no one turned in. The police officers were excessively nervous, the captain was in despair, and the sailors were rather more uneasy than sailors ordinarily are with "the shore on board".

To me, of course, the accident was an acceptable respite and even offered a faint chance of escape. If the ship should go to pieces, so much the better. I was an excellent swimmer and had no doubt that, with the aid of some buoyant object, such as the cask on which I was seated, I could keep afloat until some passing vessel should pick me up. I turned over in my mind the exact procedure that I should follow in such a contingency, and considered whether, with the support of the floating cask, I could possibly reach the shore. And then, from the possibility of the ship breaking up, my mind passed naturally to the consideration of what I should do if she did not break up.

The tide turned at about one o'clock. The swirling and bubbling against the port side gradually died away and after an interval began to make itself heard from the starboard side. I looked about me with a new interest. The police officers were seated on the main hatch – no more camp stools for them! – hunched up and evidently dozing. The captain had retired temporarily to his cabin; the crew were sitting about, half or wholly asleep, and, in the first confusion, my guard had abandoned his post and had forgotten to return.

The only boat that the ship carried rested in chocks on the booms, with a canvas cover laced on and a pile of raffle heaped on top. It would take a quarter of an hour at least to get her in the water. The tide was now running up strongly, and a mile or so away upstream I could see a light that winked in and out at regular intervals – a gas-buoy, beyond all doubt, for I had seen it in the same place ever since we ran aground. That would furnish a guiding mark and perhaps a support as well.

Why not? It was a bit of a risk; but anything was better than a Russian prison.

With a last look round, I quickly slipped off my boots and then rose silently, and, picking up the little empty cask, crept stealthily across to the bulwark. With some difficulty, I climbed up and got astride the rail; but I suppose that, being hampered by the cask, I must have made some slight noise, for, just as I was getting my other leg over, some idiot of a seaman saw me and began to bleat aloud. Instantly, of course, every imbecile on deck started to his feet and a universal howl arose. There was no time for nice manœuvres. I dropped the cask into the sea, and, catching my heels on the top side moulding, took a header and struck out underwater towards the ship's stern, round which I had noticed the tide stream swirling strongly. When I came up, I was just abreast of the rudder; and the first thing of which I was sensible was a rapid succession of pistol shots, mingled with a vocal hubbub such as one might have expected to hear at the foot of the Tower of Babel on Saturday afternoon when the hands were being paid off. I clung to the rudder for a few moments to get a good deep breath, and watched the cask – which was apparently the mark of the not very expert shooters – as it gyrated in the eddy and slowly drifted out of range. Then I dived below again and struck out in the same direction, keeping under the surface as long as my breath would hold out.

When I came up again the ship was about twenty yards away and receding rapidly as I was borne along on the tide. The marksmen were still popping away briskly, and, by the instantaneous flashes and the glimmer of the anchor light, I could make out a huddle of heads at the bulwark rail, all apparently staring at the cask, by which I judged that no one had yet succeeded in hitting it. I also got a glimpse of a party of men up on the booms clearing away the raffle from the boat; and then, as a further precaution, I quietly sank below the surface for another half-minute.

On my third emergence the ship had faded to a large, dark shape relieved by the yellow spark of the anchor light. Occasional flashes accompanied by sharp reports still burst out sporadically, but their diminishing frequency suggested that ammunition was running short. The excited babbling of many voices and a loud clatter suggested that strenuous efforts were being made to get the boat ready for launching, and hinted to me that any attempt on my part to recover the cask would be unwise; that it would, in fact, be desirable to get as far from it as possible. Accordingly, taking my direction from the ship's anchor light, I struck out across the tide, paddling very gently, however, to avoid unnecessary fatigue.

Gradually the ship faded away into the darkness until her position could be made out only by the glimmer of her anchor light. The pistol shots ceased and the clamour from her deck grew faint with the distance. I ceased from all effort beyond what was necessary barely to keep my head above the surface and let myself just drift on the tide. I was, so far, not at all fatigued. The water was comparatively warm and the slight ripple on the surface was not enough to cause any difficulty.

Still, it was not quite what I had bargained for. I had intended to float quietly, hanging on to the cask until daylight came and someone saw me. Now I must keep afloat by my own efforts until I was picked up or found something to support me. And realizing this with sudden anxiety – for hitherto I had been entirely occupied in getting away from the ship – I turned my attention to the floating light that I had seen from the deck. From my low position, with my eyes but a few inches from the surface of the water, I had at first lost sight of it entirely, but now I began to catch an occasional glimpse of it over my low horizon; and I was rather dismayed to notice that it did not seem appreciably nearer. Apparently it was a good deal farther off than I had thought.

The time slipped away; it seemed to me that hours passed. And still I drifted on, encompassed by an illimitable dark void, with the inky ripples playing about my chin. An awesome silence was over the dark sea, a silence that seemed the more intense for the lonesome sounds that disturbed it at long intervals; the hoot of some distant steamer's whistle, or the melancholy scream of a gull. The light of the gas-buoy was now continuously visible, winking monotonously every few seconds, but still it looked little nearer than before. And now a new anxiety arose. Was I approaching the buoy in a direct line? If not, I should be swept past it by the tide, and then – but I refused to think of this contingency. Keeping my face steadily towards the light I maintained a slow and easy breaststroke. I could do no more in the absence of a second light to give the direction of my movement.

Quite suddenly, as it seemed, the light loomed up big and bright. I could see the lantern distinctly. I could even see the shutter. And, as I stopped paddling for a moment, I could see something less agreeable. The light seemed to be passing across to my left. In a few moments more I should be swept past it and my last hope would be gone; and as I realized this, I realized, too, that I was growing numb and weak. Setting my teeth, I turned on my side and struck out with all my remaining strength towards the space to the left of the buoy.

The lantern towered above me. The great black shape rushed out of the darkness, looking weird and gigantic. It closed in nearer and nearer – and then began to sweep across in front of me. With a gasp of despair, I gave a final stroke, and, as the great shadowy form swept past, I clutched at it frantically and my fingers closed on a handful of slippery seaweed.

The common bladderwrack (*Fucus vesiculosus*) is not a handsome plant, but to me it is, and will ever be, more precious than the Rose of Sharon or the Lily of the Valley; for its crackling, leathery fronds stood between me and a watery grave. As I grasped that slimy handful, the tide swung me round and bumped me against the buoy and my free hand clutched a barnacle-encrusted iron bar. That bar, I found, was the bottom rung of a rough ladder, fitted for the convenience of the Trinity House men when they are recharging the buoy or attending to the lantern; and, having made this discovery, I reached for the next rung and thankfully hauled myself up, dripping and shivering, to the shoulder of the buoy.

It was bitterly cold – at least, it seemed so; though the breeze that blew on my drenched clothing was really warm. But I was safe; unless the *Anna*'s boat should come so far and hit this particular spot, which was infinitely unlikely. So I sat, with chattering teeth, physically wretched though secure and cheerful, on the flat shoulder of the buoy, with my feet on the ladder, holding on by the cage that supported the lantern; on which cage I was able to make out the mystical inscription: "East Spaniard."

I had resigned myself to the idea of hanging on until daylight should enable me to signal to some passing vessel. Without hope or expectation of release I clung to the iron cage, growing colder and colder, and listened to the wash of the ripples against the buoy and the monotonous click of the shutter in the lantern above me; these, and the occasional scream of a gull being the only sounds that broke the dreary silence, until I had been on the buoy for what seemed like several hours. Then my ear caught some new sounds, thin and faint at first, but gradually increasing in distinctness as if their source was approaching; the unmistakable sound of oars working in wide tholes, with long pauses filled by heavy splashes, bumpings and the murmur of voices, as yet afar off. I listened intently. Though wildly improbable, it was not actually impossible that this might be the *Anna*'s boat still searching for a cask and a fugitive; and if it should be, I might have to get into the water again to dodge behind the buoy.

The sounds approached very gradually, with short spells of rowing and long intervals of bumping, splashing and the mumble of undistinguishable talk. But suddenly the silence of the sea was broken by a fine brassy voice lifting itself up in song:

"Oh! I love to think of the day when I was young,
Tiddley um!"

My heart leapt. Sweeter to me than a siren's song – and much more to the purpose – were those homely words, bellowed out in a voice like that of an adolescent calf. Gathering my strength for a mighty shout, I let off a feeble, quavering croak.

"Boat ahoy!"

The caroller stopped short – on the word "Tiddley" – and exclaimed:

"J'ear that, Joe?"

"Ay," replied a second voice. "That was someone a-hailing, that was."

I croaked again; my chattering teeth giving a fine tremolo effect.

"Hallo!" roared the first man. "Who are you?"

"I'm overboard," I squawked; "hanging on the gas-buoy."

"Right-O, mate," was the cheering rejoinder. "Hang on a bit longer until I gets my anchor up."

There was a brief pause, a splash and a rumble, and then I heard the oars plied with a will. The sounds rapidly grew louder, and presently the light of the buoy's lantern fell on a boat, urged forward by two men in yellow oilskins who stood up at their oars facing towards me. As she swept alongside, the forward rower helped me to scramble off the buoy – for I was stiff with the cold – and then pushed clear.

"Where are you from, mate?" he asked.

I replied, as well as my chattering jaws would let me, "Ca-cac-anterbury."

"Lor!" was the astonished comment of my rescuer.

"What's he say, Tom?" asked the other man.

"Says he dropped overboard from Canterbury."

"My eye!" exclaimed the other. "He must have had some way on him."

Not wishing to mislead my friends, I attempted to explain, but failed miserably, for my teeth were rattling like castanets. Then the hospitable Tom peeled off his long oilskin coat, and having hustled me into it, clapped his sou'wester on my head and tied the flaps over my ears.

"It's lucky for you as we happened to come down on the night tide," he remarked as we paddled back to the fishing ground – my friends were whelkers – "'tain't often as we do. We likes the daylight for to pick up our floats. Feelin' a bit warmer?"

I was feeling much warmer and somewhat like a pudding in its cloth, for the oilskin was practically air-tight and "kept in all the juices", as the cooks say. And as I revived I gave my friends a full and true account of my adventures, to which they listened open-mouthed in the intervals of hauling up and re-baiting the whelk pots. Very soon a faint glow in the eastern sky heralded the dawn and brightened by degrees until the calm sea was enveloped in a primrose-coloured haze, out of which slowly emerged the shadowy form of the barquentine, about three miles distant. Tom was the first to observe her, and pointed her out with gleeful derision.

"There's the old Rooshian basket, Joe. D'ye see? Why, blow me, if they ain't been and sat her on the Pan Sand! Haw! Haw!" (The joy of the angels over the repentant sinner is feeble compared with that of the local expert over the blundering stranger.) "Seems to be puttin' off a boat too."

They were; and I watched that boat with some anxiety, wondering how many more whelk pots remained to be dealt with. At first a mere speck, she crept steadily towards us on the flowing tide until I was able to make out details; the rag of sail, like a charwoman's apron, the two strenuous rowers and three men in the stern. These latter interested me especially. They did not look like sailors; and when a gleam of sunlight, reflected from the face of one of them, revealed a pair of spectacles, I had no doubt that I was looking on Herr von Bommel.

"Last pot, Tom," said Joe, hauling it into the boat and picking out the misguided whelks. "Them Rooshians seem to be a-hailin' of us."

I had already noticed the fact. Herr von Bommel was standing up waving a handkerchief and over the sea came a sound like the voice of an asthmatic merman.

The last pot was baited and sunk; the anchor was hove up and the tiller shipped; and then the great brown lug slid up the mast. The *Anna*'s boat was now hardly a couple of hundred yards distant and her crew and passengers were bellowing in concert. Three foreign gentlemen wanted a passage to Whitstable, and wanted it badly. But the fishermen took no notice; and when Tom grasped the tiller and Joe hauled in the sheet, the big lug filled and the water began to tinkle past the run. The *Anna*'s crew raised a final, despairing howl and the rowers strained at their oars. But our boat, though she hailed from Whitstable, was an East-country craft, deep, beamy and double-ended; and when an East-coast "Crabber" fills her enormous sail, you can take off your hat to anything astern, except, perhaps, a Deal galley-punt. When I climbed up the steep beach by Whitstable Pier and peeled off the oilskin coat before making a run for the station, the *Anna*'s boat was but a grey spot far out on the sea.

Some three hours later I sat by the coffee-room window of the Falstaff Inn looking out lazily through the wire blind. A hot bath, a dry suit and a colossal breakfast had induced a placid and contemplative frame of mind which inclined me indolently to observe the world without. And as I looked, three men crawled wearily along the opposite side of the street, having apparently come from the station. Opposite the inn, they paused, and the middle one, who wore spectacles, produced a scrap of paper from his pocket, over which they all pored with knitted brows. Then, as with one accord, they all yawned prodigiously; the spectacled one pocketed the paper and, slowly and languidly, they all went their way.

By which signs I gathered that the "secret code" of the Harp and Cross was still undeciphered.

CHAPTER THREE
The Secret Chamber

It is my firm and unalterable conviction that Izaak Walton was an impostor. I am thinking, at the moment, of his observations on the Fordidge trout, a mythical fish, "near the bigness of a salmon", which is said to inhabit the River Stour in Kent. Very ingenious and abstruse are old Izaak's explanations of the suspicious fact that none of these leviathans of the deep have ever been "caught with an angle"; but I can give a much simpler one. There is no such fish. That was the conclusion that I reached after a couple of evening's angling from the boat belonging to the Royal George Inn, where I was now lodging; having had but a single bite all the time, and even then only hauled up a fat-headed gudgeon who grinned in my face and then dropped off the hook and swam away. Fordidge trout, indeed! "I don't believe there's no sech a person" – to borrow Mrs Gamp's immortal phrase.

Not that it really mattered to me. If it had, I suppose I should not have baited my hook with three-quarters of a yard of garden worm. But the old tub of a boat was restful, and secure, too. I couldn't very well get pounced on unawares so long as I was moored in midstream; and that was a consideration after what I had gone through. So I sat in the boat, ostensibly to fish, but actually to meditate.

I had plenty to meditate about. The material had been accumulating since I came to Canterbury a little over a week ago. In that short time I had been arrested by an English detective and liberated; arrested again by the Russian Secret Police, and had escaped.

And now, to my certain knowledge, the Russian Police ere still lurking in the neighbourhood, and the British detective had developed the companionable qualities of Mary's little lamb. Wherever I went, that detective was sure to go. I was continually meeting him; and what made it worse was the offensive fiction that he kept of not observing me.

Sergeant Burbler's proceedings were a puzzle to me. Did he still believe that I was connected with the gang of foreign criminals who had sheltered in the old manor house? It seemed impossible. But there was another explanation of his adhesiveness. The sergeant and I both believed that somewhere in that old manor house was concealed the treasure deposited three centuries ago by Simon Glynn; and each of us suspected the other of having some private information on the subject. Could it be Simon Glynn's hoard to which I was indebted for so much of the sergeant's society? It was impossible to say. And here I raised my eyes – and beheld the sergeant himself, angling from the bank.

He was at his old game, pretending not to see me. Which was ridiculous; for there I was a most visible reality. But I wasn't going to have any more of this nonsense. I watched him stick a lump of cheese on his hook – in the hope, perhaps, that the Fordidge trout favoured the purine-free diet – and when he had made his cast, I addressed him by name. Then he pretended that he didn't know me. Now I am no advocate for laxity in regard to etiquette; but when two men have rolled round a room together, have dusted the floor with one another, have prodded one another in the abdomen and pulled out handfuls of one another's hair, I say that for either of them to pretend that they are not acquainted is mere paltry snobbery. I wasn't going to have it. But, as he seemed to have got a bite, I waited to renew my attack.

I saw his line tighten. I watched him strike, and then begin to wind in his winch as if he were playing a little barrel organ. I saw him reach out stealthily for his landing net and crane over the bank, and still I kept a discreet silence. It was only when I had seen him disengage a waterlogged boot from his hook and rebait that I ventured to reopen conversation.

"I'm getting quite used to being arrested now," I remarked.

"Oh," said Burbler. "Who's been arresting you?"

"The Russian Police have had another go at me," I replied.

"Oh," said Burbler. "Why did they let you go?"

"They didn't. I let myself go."

That excited his curiosity so far that he asked for particulars. I lashed the rudder over so as to give the boat a cast inshore and proceeded to give him a detailed account of those astonishing events that culminated in my escape from the Russian timber ship. He was profoundly interested in my adventures; there was no doubt of that. So much so that when I had finished my story I ventured to ask him a question or two about himself.

"You don't suppose that that gang of crooks is still in this neighbourhood, do you?"

"Have I ever said I did?" was his Scottesque reply.

"No: but as you are remaining in neighbourhood yourself, I thought that, perhaps — well, that you might have some object in doing so."

"Sounds reasonable," he admitted, dryly. Then, after a brief pause, he remarked: "You seem to be putting in a bit of time in the neighbourhood yourself."

"Yes," I answered. "I have to superintend some repairs of Elham Manor House."

"You're taking your time about it," said he.

"Oh, I haven't begun. I'm waiting to consult with our new tenant and he hasn't turned up yet. I can't write to him because I don't know where he is staying. He's an American — Mr Jezreel P Damper — and these rich Americans are rather erratic in their movements."

"What sort of repairs are you going to do?" Burbler asked carelessly.

Now, here I seemed to see an opportunity for pumping the taciturn detective as to his object in shadowing me in this singular manner. Accordingly, I replied, putting some slight tension on the actual facts:

"The repairs will probably involve some structural alterations. It's an old house, you know, and it may need to be modernized a little."

He took the bait with avidity – unlike the Fordidge trout. His sour visage brightened with an ingratiating smile as he exclaimed enthusiastically:

"How very interesting! Excuse my curiosity, but old buildings are rather a hobby of mine. Have you decided on any particular structural alterations?"

"No," I replied, cramming the bait into his gizzard with both hands, so to speak; "I have hardly looked at the house yet."

"Really!" he exclaimed. "Really! Might I just step into your boat? More convenient for conversation, you know." And when I had edged inshore and let him scramble on board with his neglected tackle, he continued: "So you haven't really looked over the house yet? I wonder at that. Don't you think it would be wise to make a thorough inspection so as to be ready for your tenant when he arrives?"

As a matter of fact I had thought so. But since my two encounters with the Russian Secret Police, I had been rather shy of Elham Manor. I knew that they were watching it and that they had once obtained access to it; and the lonely old house was an awkward place in which to be caught by gentry of that kind. I explained this to the sergeant – omitting to mention, however, that I had taken to carrying a revolver since my last adventure. Again he rose joyously like a hungry perch.

"I quite agree with you, Mr Cobb" – the rascal let my name drop inadvertently. "It would be most unwise of you to venture into the house alone. But if you want to look over it, I shall be delighted to accompany you: and, as I always carry a regulation revolver, you will be perfectly safe. What do you say?"

I didn't quite know what to say. I wanted to look over the house but I didn't particularly want Burbler; but still less did I want to be haled off to some Russian gaol. In the end I accepted Burbler's offer, resolving to keep an eye on him in case he had any private information about Simon Glynn's treasure.

"When would you like me to come with you?" he asked briskly.

"Any time you like," said I.

"Well, why not now? There are several hours of daylight left."

He tried to disguise his eagerness and failed miserably. Obviously he was, as Mr Bumble would have said, "on broken bottles" with anxiety to start.

"Don't you want to have a try for the other boot?" I asked callously.

He cast a baleful glance at his last catch, which lay stranded on the bank, and, without reply other than a sour smile, proceeded to heave up our little hairpin of an anchor. A few minutes later we landed at the stairs belonging to the Royal George and passed unmolested through the garden and taproom out into the road.

As we trudged along together many thoughts passed through my mind. Obviously the sergeant was hot on the scent of Simon Glynn's hoard and proposed to use me as a cat's-paw to hook it out of its hiding place. But the question was, how much did he know? Had he some information about it that I had not? If so, I must watch him closely. As to my own knowledge on the subject, it was summed up in a passage in Boteler's "Manor Houses of Kent", which I had looked up at the Public Library in Canterbury. It read thus:

"In 1734, during some repairs, an aumbry was discovered behind the panelling of the dining room and in this was found a curious silver mirror, probably Glynn's own handiwork, the frame of which bore this strange inscription:

"A harp and a Cross and good redd golde
Beneath ye cross with ye harp full nigh,
Ankores three atte ye foot of a tree
And a Maid from ye sea on high.
Take itt. 'Tis thine. Others have stepped over. Simon Glynn, 1683."

"The meaning of this inscription has never been ascertained. The gateposts of Elham Manor House bear a harp and a cross respectively, and above the porch is a statue of a young Puritan lady, presumably Mistress Glynn. Hence it has been inferred that the lines refer to a treasure buried under the gatepost which bears the cross; but repeated excavations have failed to discover any such treasure.

"Simon Glynn is said to have had a mania for secret hiding places. Tradition speaks of several in the manor house – in one of which Axell, the regicide, is said to have lain concealed for some time – but their position (if they ever existed) has been forgotten. Perhaps Glynn's hoard is still lying in some forgotten, secret strongroom."

Thus the learned Boteler. He hadn't very much to tell excepting that the treasure was still "untrove". But one thing was clear to me: the people who had dug under the gatepost were fools. If the meaning of the doggerel had been as simple as that, Simon might as well have laid his treasure in the road for the first passing imbecile to pick up. There was some deeper meaning in that crude jingle and it must be my business to fathom it – unless Burbler had done so already.

These reflections brought us to the gates of the manor house; and here the sergeant halted to gaze reflectively at the traces of the "repeated excavations" and at the statue in its niche above the porch.

"I wonder who she was," he said, nodding at the statue. "Do you think she looks like an Englishwoman?"

It was a transparent question. He was clearly thinking of "a Maid from the sea on high". But, as it was not my business to enlighten him, I expressed ambiguous doubts, and we passed up the flagged path to the main door, into which I inserted the key.

For some time we rambled rather aimlessly through the rooms, waking the echoes with our footfalls on the massive oak floors. It was an eerie place, full of odd corners, little flights of stairs and great built-in cupboards. No two rooms seemed to be on the same level. It was a step or two up or down every time. And every room appeared to be set at an angle to its fellow; a wasteful arrangement as regards space, but an excellent one for a builder whose hobby happened to be secret hiding places.

I watched Burbler narrowly – and found him watching me. But all the same, his eye travelled inquisitively towards each cupboard or closet that we passed.

"Don't you think this old panelling is rather a mistake?" said he, rapping at it with his knuckles. "Makes the place so dark, you know."

"It does," I agreed. "Perhaps I may have some of it down and plaster the walls if our tenant agrees." This, I regret to say, was a sheer falsehood. Nothing would have induced me to mutilate the fine old house. But the tarradiddle served its purpose, for Burbler exclaimed excitedly:

"Shall you really? I hope you will allow me to be present when it is done. I am so very much interested in old buildings. And besides," he added, as a brilliant afterthought, "it is quite possible that there may be some of the stolen property hidden here. That St Petersburg-Chicago gang used this house for some time, you know."

"You don't suppose they are hanging about here still, do you?" I asked.

Burbler looked about him — we were in the large drawing room at the time — and listened as if apprehensive of eavesdroppers. Then he replied:

"I don't personally. But they haven't turned up anywhere else; and my orders are to keep a watch on this house until they are run to earth or seen somewhere else. So, of course, I ought to be present when any structural alterations are made here, in case they have secreted the booty here. And, between you and me, Mr Cobb, it wouldn't be a bad plan, if you thought of doing away with that panelling, for us to take some of it down ourselves, and avoid the inconvenience of inquisitive workmen. What do you say?"

I said I would think the matter over; and at that he was content to leave it for the present. But from that moment he developed a tendency to lag behind or stray away on various pretences: and whenever he did so, there came from adjoining rooms sundry mysterious tappings, as if some gigantic woodpecker had got loose in the house. But nothing of special interest occurred until we entered a large room at the back of the building, distinguished by peculiarly fine woodwork. It was a rather uncanny room, in spite of its beauty, for its panelling was carved throughout in high relief with very realistic grotesque figures, which seemed to start out from the walls in a manner that was really quite disturbing. And more alarming still was the broad, carved oak frieze that surmounted the walls below the heavy cornice, of which the chief ornament was a row of life-size masks, each one different from the others, and all, apparently, grotesque portraits of actual persons. The aspect of those masks was most diabolical. They grinned, they scowled, they sneered, and some of them stuck out their tongues; and their eyes – represented by deep-sunk holes – seemed to leer down on us with positively devilish malice. I wouldn't have lived in that room for a thousand a year.

But this was not all. A further attraction in that ghostly apartment was a large armoire or cupboard of sepulchral aspect, built into the wall. I opened one of the folding doors and looked in; and then I shut it again rather quickly and turned away with as careless and uninterested a manner as I could assume at such short notice. For I had observed that it was fitted with massive, fixed shelves. Now everybody who knows anything about secret chambers is familiar with the cupboard with the sliding shelf that conceals a movable panel. Of course I couldn't tell whether any of these shelves would slide out; but they looked uncommonly likely, and I thought I should prefer to try when I was alone. So I turned away and endeavoured to distract the sergeant's attention from the cupboard.

But, bless you! he didn't want any distracting. Not he! The one plain and palpable fact was that Sergeant Burbler hadn't noticed the cupboard at all. He stared at the walls and the ceiling and the floor, but the cupboard had totally escaped his observation. He never looked at it – after the first glance.

We sauntered through a doorway into an adjoining room; a smallish chamber with no outlet save by the door by which we had entered, unless there was some concealed door in the panelling. Here we remained for a minute or two rapping at the wainscot and examining the window seat, and then Burbler strolled back into the other room "to have another look at those quaint figures on the walls". I continued my investigations, which presently brought me to the disproportionately large open fireplace, the brick back of which I proceeded to test by a series of interrogatory thumps. It all sounded solid enough, but when I had delivered an extra heavy thump on the left-hand side, to my astonishment the brickwork itself began to move. A square patch, cleverly concealed by the joints between the bricks, swung round slightly on its centre, being evidently balanced on a pivot. I hastily closed it by pushing at the opposite end and then stole towards the door, with the intention of luring the sergeant to some distant part of the house and then returning alone to investigate. But Burbler was beforehand with me. As I approached the door it closed softly and a bolt was shot on the outside. The perfidious detective had bolted me in.

It was a quaint situation. With a self-satisfied grin I gave a thump or two on the door for the sake of appearances and then stole on tiptoe back to the fireplace. A hearty shove at the left side of the chimney back sent the panel of brickwork swinging on its pivot and disclosed a dark opening, Before entering I cautiously examined the mechanism, which was simple enough. The false brickwork was fixed to massive oak planks which revolved, as I have said, on pivots. There was no secret spring, but there was a strong bolt on the inside with which a fugitive could fix the panel immovably, and a handle with which to pull it open from within. Massive as it was, it moved quite easily and without a sound, which seemed strange, considering the long years of disuse – until one examined the pivot and found it smooth and bright and anointed with oil that was certainly not two and a half centuries old.

I stepped into the opening and shut the panel, fixing it with the bolt and reflecting gleefully on the surprise that Burbler would get when he came to let me out of the room. Striking a wax match, I saw a tiny brick staircase, not more than two feet wide, apparently built in the thickness of the wall, and began to ascend it with extreme caution – for one has to beware of "mousetrap staircases" in these old hiding holes. At the top was a passage or gallery of the same width, and on the right hand a small door. The latter I pushed open and entered a small chamber, about five feet by ten, well lighted from above by a false chimney, up which I peered, and caught the eye of a starling who was perched on top. The little room was furnished with an antique folding table, a fixed bench and a fine oaken chair – which must have been built in the room, since it was too large to come up the stairs, and which would have electrified Wardour Street. And that was all – excepting two blatantly modern cabin trunks.

At those two trunks I stared open-mouthed; and especially at the smaller of the two. For I had seen it before. It was, in fact, the identical trunk that I had seen when I first visited the old manor house. I knew what it contained. It was crammed with the costly booty of those rascals, the St Petersburg-Chicago gang. Diamonds, rubies, emeralds and golden baubles – a bushel or so of them – were here before me. They were mine for the mere taking! What an opportunity for a dishonest man! But I am not a dishonest man. And, incidentally, the trunk was now secured with a massive padlock.

When I had tested the weight of the two trunks, and found the smaller one considerably the heavier, I came out of the room and proceeded to explore the gallery. It was not quite dark. On the right-hand wall were a number of little circles of light; and as I stole silently along the brick floor, I was able to trace these patches of light to their source, which was a series of little round holes in the left-hand wall. A single glance at these told me what they were. They were the eye-holes of those appalling masks in the large room, and their purpose was obviously to enable a fugitive to watch and listen to the talk of pursuers or traitors in the room below.

I applied my eye to one of the holes and found that it commanded quite a large circular area; and at the centre of the circle was Detective-Sergeant Burbler. He had noticed the cupboard at last. In fact he had both the doors wide open and was tugging frantically at the shelves.

But he didn't seem to have had much luck. He had, apparently, begun at the bottom and tried them all in turn; and none of them had budged a hair's breadth. I watched him with a pitying smile. He had now come to the top shelf but one, and, as it was a little above his reach, he had to stand on a lower shelf to get hold of it. He tried it first quite gently, then more vigorously, and, as it still refused to move, he planted one foot against an upper shelf and tugged with might and main. And then it did move; and so did he. He shot away like a spring-jack and came down on his back with a bang that shook the house and the detached shelf clutched triumphantly in his paws.

He got up, stroking himself delicately and soliloquizing not at all delicately. And at that moment a quick footfall was heard approaching from an adjacent room. Burbler snatched up the shelf and made frenzied efforts to replace it. But if it had been difficult to get it out, it was impossible to get it back. It certainly entered its grooves – just enough to prevent the doors from shutting; and there it stuck, refusing to move either way. And there it still was when a stranger entered the room and swam into the magic circle of my field of vision.

A stern and wrathful-looking man was the newcomer, with a red face and a very large chin, and his manner was not more conciliatory than his appearance.

"What the deuce is the meaning of this, sir?" he demanded in a rasping voice and with a distinct American accent. "Who are you? and what are you doing in this house?"

I have never seen a man look such an unutterable fool as Burbler did at that moment. But he pulled himself together a little and retorted:

"I might ask the same question. Who are *you?* and what are *you* doing here?"

"You might," said the stranger. "I can quite believe it of you. But I'll tell you who I am. I am the tenant of this house and my name is Damper, if you want to know; Jezreel P Damper."

"Oh," said Burbler; "I've heard Mr Cobb speak of you."

"Have you?" replied Damper. "Well, who are you, anyway?"

"I'm a police officer, sir," said Burbler, with an abortive attempt to be impressive. "I have instructions to watch this house, as certain suspicious characters are known to have harboured in it."

"Were you 'instructed' to destroy the landlord's fixtures?" asked Damper, glaring at the displaced shelf.

Burbler began a windy explanation with certain references to stolen property, but Damper cut him short.

"Is Mr Cobb in the house?" he asked.

"He was here a minute ago," replied Burbler. "He went into the next room. Perhaps he's there still." It did seem rather likely under the circumstances; but when the sergeant had slipped back the rusty bolt and looked into the room he evidently got a severe shock, for he came back looking very blank and puzzled.

"He seems to have gone away," he mumbled, "but I expect he'll be back presently."

"Now see here," said Damper. "That door was bolted and there isn't any other. I guess you've been dreaming about Mr Cobb."

"I assure you, sir," protested Burbler, "that he was here a minute ago; and I have his full authority to search the premises thoroughly."

Of course, that was a barefaced untruth, and I couldn't allow it to pass. Lifting up my voice, I shouted:

"Nothing of the kind, sergeant. I gave you no authority whatever."

My word! but that gave Burbler a start! He jumped like a cat that has sat down on an exploding cracker, and tried to look in all directions at once. But if Burbler was startled, Mr Damper was positively petrified; and, to be sure, it is a little disturbing to an incoming tenant to hear voices issuing apparently from the walls or ceiling.

"Would you mind stepping this way, Mr Cobb," said the sergeant, after looking into the cupboard and up the chimney. I thought it about time to make my appearance on the scene, and accordingly retraced my steps along the passage, down the stairs and out through the concealed entrance, and finally shattered the sergeant's nerves by emerging from the room which he had just seen to be empty.

Of course, Burbler had to be told about the box of "swag", so I gave him the information forthwith; on which he dived jubilantly into the smaller room. But Mr Damper was much less pleased. He followed us with a distinctly worried expression and finally remarked:

"This is extremely disagreeable for me, Mr Cobb. The presence of this stolen property in the house naturally suggests that the thieves themselves are not far off and that they have access to the premises."

"Oh, you needn't be uneasy, sir," said Burbler. "We shall soon clear the rascals out of this. Now, Mr Cobb, if you please."

I pushed the square of brickwork open, and entering, preceded the sergeant up the stairs to the secret chamber. He pounced gleefully on the smaller trunk and proceeded to drag it away down the stairs, haughtily refusing my proffered assistance. I saw him struggle out with it through the opening, I heard him dump it down on the floor, and then he returned for the larger trunk.

"Hadn't I better lend you a hand?" said I.

"Be good enough, sir, not to interfere," he replied stiffly. "This is official business."

I watched him lumber out with the trunk and heard him clatter down the stairs, which were now quite dark, owing, as I supposed, to his having pulled the panel to as he returned. When he reached the bottom there was a long pause, filled in with a sound of fumbling and low-toned profane soliloquy. At length he called out, with a sudden return to civility:

"Just step down here, Mr Cobb. You know how this thing goes better than I do."

I skipped down the narrow stairs with alacrity and a little uneasiness.

"It's quite simple," I said. "You just catch hold of this handle and pull."

"That's what I've been doing," growled Burbler.

I seized the handle and pulled at it vigorously; but the false door was as immovable as the Great Pyramid. Apparently some secret catch had released itself. I lit a wax match and examined the back of the panel, but without finding anything that could explain the phenomenon, while Burbler shouted to Mr Damper to give a good shove from the outside.

"Are you there, Mr Damper?" roared Burbler.

Apparently he was not, or was unable to hear us, for we heard no reply. Then we both scampered up the stairs in a mighty twitter – for it was really an exceedingly awkward situation – and made for the gallery, where each of us glued his eye to one of the peepholes preparatory to calling out. And then – Oh! what a sight was there, my countrymen! Mr Jezreel P Damper was certainly in full view, and no longer stern-faced and worried, but bland and smiling. But there were two other gentlemen also; one of whom – who looked, as to his hair, like a professional pianist – was at that very moment hoisting the precious cabin trunk on to his shoulder with the other man's aid.

"Hi! there!" shouted Burbler. "What are you doing with that trunk?"

Mr Damper looked up with a gracious smile. "That you, Burbey?" he asked. "Sorry I can't see your face. Let me introduce you to my two friends, Polopsky and Schneider. Turn round, Polly, and let the gentlemen see your beautiful hair."

"You infernal scoundrel!" shrieked Burbler. "I suppose you are Jacob Mifflin?"

"You've hit it, sonny. You have indeed. Right in the middle. Clever boy!" and Mr Damper – or Mifflin – made a show, in pantomime, of patting Burbler on the head.

"You're not going to leave us locked up here to starve, are you?" demanded the sergeant.

"Well," replied Mifflin, "we just hate leaving you behind, sonny, but I guess we haven't enough accommodation to take you with us. But you'll be happy enough. You've got furnished apartments and board – there's a week's provisions in that trunk – and we shall send on the keys of the house with a little note to Mr Cobb's agent in Canterbury."

"When?" I shouted.

"Quite soon, Mr Cobb. Perhaps we may send them tonight. We don't wish to inconvenience you. Oh, and there's another little matter, Mr Cobb. I inferred from the interesting conversation that I happened to overhear just now in the big drawing room that you and the sergeant are looking around for some antique curios. Well, you'll find some exceedingly remarkable ones in that very room, which we are leaving behind for want of transport facilities. The right-hand column under the arch there is a concealed door. It isn't fastened. Give a good pull at the left corner and it will come open. The contents of the hiding place are yours for the taking. And now I must really tear myself away. Ta-ta, dear friends!"

He took off his hat with a flourish and made us an elaborate bow; and then he moved away out of our circle of vision and we heard his footsteps gradually die away in the distance.

"Well," said Burbler, unglueing his eye at length, "this is a pretty mess that you've got us into!"

I was too disgusted to reply. Here I was, sealed up in this infernal hiding hole, my very life dependent on the doubtful goodwill of a band of ruffians. And why? Simply because this inquisitive booby of a policeman must go poking his nose into places where he had no business. It was abominable.

The sergeant and I crept out of the gallery, and our first proceeding was to fetch up the provision trunk. It was secured only with spring catches, and when we had unfastened these we found an ample supply of food and drink, including a gallon can of beer and another of water, all neatly packed in compartments. Apparently the gang had intended to remain in residence here for some time longer and had been compelled to migrate only by Burbler's ridiculous prowlings and his absurd suggestions – overheard by them – of structural alterations. We inaugurated our tenancy by a good meal, and, as the light was now failing, we lit one of the candles that we had found in the trunk and fell to discussing our unsatisfactory situation.

"If those scoundrels don't take any measures to get us released," said I, "we shall have to make some effort to break out or else climb up the chimney."

Burbler held the candle aloft and peered up the smooth-sided shaft.

"No," he said, shaking his head; "there's nothing to hold on by. But Mifflin will keep his word, or else why should he have told us of that stuff in the hiding hole? I wonder what it is, by the way. Can't be of much value, or they wouldn't have left it behind."

I agreed that this was self-evident, and we returned to the question of a possible escape but without reaching any conclusion, though we talked far into the night. Finally we blew out the candle and settled ourselves for the night, Burbler on the fixed bench and I in the arm-chair.

It was about ten o'clock on the following morning when the sergeant and I, sitting disconsolately in our prison, were thrilled by a hollow "boom" that sounded infinitely distant.

"By gum!" exclaimed Burbler, "that was the front door!"

He sprang up and made for the gallery like a rabbit scuttling for its burrow, and I followed. Very soon the heavenly sound of a pair of creaky boots was borne to our ears and then a tremulous voice called out: "Mr Cobb! Are you here?"

"Yes!" I howled. "I'm here!"

As a guide to my exact locality, I must admit that this was not particularly lucid. But the boots continued to approach, and at length there appeared in my circle of vision a very nervous-looking young man, who stared about him apprehensively as he walked.

"Where are you, sir?" he asked.

"Here!" roared Burbler; on which the young man started violently and began to turn round like a joint of meat on a roasting-jack, staring at the walls as he turned.

"Would you go into the next room," said I, "and see if there is anything against the back of the fireplace?"

"Yessir!" he replied; and away he went like a man in a dream. But he was back in a few moments with a simple and encouraging report.

"There's a thick walking stick, sir, jammed under the chimney breast. Shall I remove it, sir?"

"If you please," I answered, and Burbler and I made our way back along the gallery and down the little staircase. As we reached the bottom, I grasped the handle and gave a tentative pull. Oh, joy! Oh, unutterable relief! It yielded at once, and the panel of brickwork swung readily open. Our imprisonment was at an end. As I stepped out, I saw through the open doorway that estimable young man addressing himself to the ceiling of the next room.

"I've removed the stick, sir."

"Thank you," said I; on which he spun round with a smothered cry. But he recovered himself sufficiently to advance to meet us and hold out a bunch of keys and a note.

"Mr Damper's keys, sir, and a note for you. Can I do anything more for you?"

"No, thank you," I replied; and as he bustled away I opened the note, which Burbler undisguisedly read over my shoulder. It was unsigned and read as follows:

"I have kept my word, you see, like a burglar and a gentleman. Tell Burbey he needn't trouble about us; we're clean away. And don't forget those curios. It's the right-hand column that opens."

"I wonder what the stuff is," said Burbler. "We may as well go and see, as we're here. Don't-cher think so?"

I did, though, to speak the truth, my enthusiasm in respect of hiding holes was not quite what it had been; and accordingly we made our way to the drawing room as it was now called. There was no difficulty in finding the "column"; which was not a column at all but a Corinthian pilaster of carved oak; one of a pair that supported an elliptical arch against the end wall. Following Mifflin's directions, Burbler seized the left-hand corner and gave a sharp pull, whereupon the whole shaft between the capital and the plinth opened, forming a tall, narrow door, and disclosing an extremely narrow flight of steps.

Burbler was extraordinarily polite. He not only held the door open for me to enter first, he actually remained outside to keep guard, as I observed on looking back from the top of the stairs. But here I had something fresh to think about, for I had come up against a solid wooden partition, and it seemed to me that vague sounds of movement and muffled voices proceeded from somewhere near at hand. I opened a small but massive door, and immediately the sounds became quite distinct; so much so that I had some thoughts of turning back and summoning the sergeant.

But pride and curiosity impelled me to advance. Passing through the doorway I traversed a short, narrow passage which brought me to another partition, in which was a square trap or door secured by a bolt. I drew back the bolt, and, pulling open the trap, which was very thick and heavy, looked into a small brick chamber, which, like my late prison, was lighted by a false chimney.

The little dungeon-like chamber contained three men; and I may say that we looked at one another with mutual astonishment. For the three prisoners were the Russian Police Agents who had kidnapped me but a short time since and who had, doubtless, believed me to be at the bottom of the sea. They looked wretched enough now, for they were all handcuffed and loosely linked together with a chain, which had been passed round a beam that crossed the cell and secured with a padlock. A sack of ship's biscuit and a couple of buckets of water had kept them from starvation but had not induced hilarious spirits.

We stared at one another in silence for a moment or two; then I ventured to ask:

"How came you to be shut in here, Herr von Bommel?"

The German's eyes flashed behind his spectacles and he exclaimed:

"Ach! It vos zat villain Mifflin, bot I shall catch him! He shall bay for zis. Ja! I shall catch him yet" (he didn't look much like it at the moment). "And you vill let us out, sir? You vill not bear a crutch for our liddle mistague?"

"Certainly, I will let you out," said I, "only you mustn't make any more mistakes, you know."

The keys of the padlock and the handcuffs hung on a nail just out of the prisoner's reach. I unlocked the padlock, and, promising to unfasten the handcuffs downstairs, took the precaution to slip out through the trap and hurry down in advance. The three prisoners soon followed; and when I had released their hands, they departed, in deep dejection and in company with Sergeant Burbler, to report the escape of the gang.

I have never seen them since – the foreign gentlemen, I mean. As to Detective-Sergeant Burbler – but that is another story, and must be reserved for another occasion.

CHAPTER FOUR

The Resurrectionists

Though I do not myself profess to be a religious man, I am a strong advocate of religion in others. It generates in them agreeable and softening conventions, it accustoms them to a dignified form of music and introduces them to an almost extinct variety of speech known as the English Language; it has even been said to influence their morals; and it does undoubtedly cause them to erect certain admirable buildings and to furnish them with organs, choirs, and other desirable, æsthetic adjuncts.

Thus reflecting, I opened the lychgate of Bouldersby Churchyard and entered. I have a strong liking for churchyards. They are quiet and restful places where one can meditate with satisfaction on the superior advantages of being alive. But I had a more particular object in this visit. I wanted to have a look at old Simon Glynn's monument in the church; and, especially, I wanted to escape from the incessant "shadowing" of Detective-Sergeant Burbler.

That officer haunted me like a familiar – a much too familiar – spirit. I couldn't get a moment to myself. And it was not affection that made him cling to me. Not at all. It was a mere, sordid desire to spy on my actions. Even now, I had only given the beggar the slip by popping behind a haystack, and he might run me to earth at any moment. I strolled up the path in the shadow of the bordering limes. The birds sang above, and from the church came, faint and muffled, the voice of a solitary chorister rehearsing a solo. I couldn't make out either the tune or the words, but I accepted the sound as an appropriate touch of local colour, like the houseleeks on the porch or the lichen on the tombstones. The south door of the church was open and, as I reached it, the sound swelled suddenly into a familiar melody and I distinguished the words:

"It stopped – short – never to go again
When the – old – man – died."

I was profoundly shocked. "Decently and in order," says the church service, and I agree most emphatically. Secular songs should not be bawled in a place of worship. Of course the singer was referring to "My Grandfather's Clock". I knew the song well, and had no patience with the mawkish, sentimental doggerel – for, after all, a drop of oil applied with a feather to the rusty bearings would have set the old rattletrap ticking again, grandfather or no grandfather. So I strode into the church frowning my disapproval.

But the frown was thrown away. The singer was but a journeyman painter, engaged in disfiguring the woodwork and carolling from mere habit. He meant no harm and was as unconscious of any impropriety as if he had been painting the outside of the bathroom window frame, while the ablutionist within hustled behind a towel. His innocence disarmed my indignation; and, besides, at the moment of my entry I got a most effectual counter-irritant; for the first object that met my eye was that fellow Burbler, staring like an idiot at a wall tablet. I was fairly taken aback. Could he have guessed that I was coming here? or had he come to grind a little private axe of his own? I should soon know, if I kept my eye on him.

"How do, Mr Cobb?" he said genially. "Having a look round? Fine old place. I was just examining this very interesting tablet."

I looked at the tablet over his shoulder. It was of no interest whatever. It merely located the carcase of a certain Major General Mulliger-Torney, HEIC, late of Elham Manor, and told a number of palpable untruths about him. "A gallant officer, and an exemplary Christian, he served with distinction in the Great Mutiny, slaying upwards of two hundred mutineers with his own hand. 'Blessed are the Peacemakers.' "

"What about it?" I asked.

"Don't you see? He lived at Elham Manor."

This was too thin. Obviously the sergeant was trying to distract my attention from something else. I glanced round and saw that something else on a wall hard by, a fine canopied monument with painted stone effigies and a tablet beneath, on which I could make out the name "Simon Glynn". I strolled over to examine it and stood awhile gazing at it in silence. There is something impressive in the naïve dignity of the mural monuments of this period; a simplicity of intention which is in no wise impaired by the elaborate and sumptuous workmanship. For some time the mere beauty and antiquarian interest of this quaintly splendid memorial engrossed my attention. Then, suddenly, I started. Now I understood why the sergeant had tried to divert my attention, and why he was now watching me like a cat. There was something more in this monument than met the eye at the first glance. Even the inscription contained arresting matter where it referred to "Margery ye onely daughter of Andreas Ozanne of ye Iland of Gurnseye Esquire"; for surely Mistress Margery Ozanne of Guernsey might fairly be described as a "Maid from the Sea".

But much more startling were the ornamental accessories of this curious monument. On either side of the surmounting finial reclined a winged figure, of which the one on the right held a harp, while the other grasped a great cross-hilted sword. Between the figures was a shield quartered with what were presumably the arms of Glynn and his wife: the one device bearing three anchors or on a field gules and the other a scallop-shell argent on a field azure, while below the shield was the motto: "God with us."

It was certainly what Dick Swiveller would have called a "staggerer". I repeated to myself the quaint doggerel that I had copied from Simon Glynn's mirror.

Well, there were all the mystic signs; the harp and the cross and the "ankores three"; and as for the "Maid from the Sea" there was Mistress Margery herself. There was only one difficulty. The "ankores three" were not at the foot of a tree, unless the great yew outside could be considered as fulfilling the condition. In all other respects the agreement was complete.

Was it possible that Glynn could have buried his treasure in the vault where his wife lay? It seemed incredible. And yet a man who could bequeath his fortune to any chance stranger who might have the wit to find it, might be capable of any eccentricity. But at this point, my reflections – and the painter's lyrical outpourings – were interrupted by a raucous voice.

"Now young man; don't you know no better than to make that there noise in a sacred hedifice?"

"Why, there ain't no harm in a-singin', is there?" protested the caroller.

"No 'arm!" exclaimed the other, whom I judged – correctly – to be the sexton. "No 'arm in a-bellerin' rye-bald songs in a place of worship? Where might you 'ave been brought up?"

"Git out," said the painter. And the hopeless irrelevancy of the rejoinder left the sexton speechless – until he perceived us; when he advanced sedately as one who scents a possible sixpence.

"Re-markable old figgers, them, sir," he said, addressing himself to me as the obvious social superior. "Wunnerful old, too: seven or eight hundred year old, so I've heerd say."

"*In*deed," said Burbler, looking daggers at me for being there – but I wasn't sensitive just then. "Most interesting. And I suppose that in those days they used to bury people in the church; under the very pavement that we're standing on?"

"No doubt they did, sir," replied the sexton; "but not them two. They are buried in the undercroft, they are. Would you like to see the place?"

It was useless to deny that we should, so we followed the sexton out of the church and round the exterior until we came to a small doorway which had once been closed by an iron gate, but was now unguarded. Entering after our guide, we descended a flight of moss-grown steps and finally reached a small crypt under the chancel. There wasn't much to see. A simple groined roof carried on four dwarf pillars; walls of unadorned masonry and a plain flagged floor. That was all; excepting that, against one wall, a square stone set in the pavement exhibited the inscription:

Margery Glynn 1662

Simon Glynn 1692

Burbler struck a wax match – for the only light that entered the crypt was that which came down the stairway – and looked long and thoughtfully at the stone. I guessed what he was thinking by the direction of my own thoughts. He was considering the difficulties of raising that stone and the tools necessary for the job: and he was wondering what there was beneath the slab. By its shape it appeared to be the cover of the entrance to a vault, and, if this were so, the difficulties would not be great. If, on the other hand, it covered a grave, there would be trouble. Digging up a grave was a rather bigger undertaking – if you will pardon the unintentional *double-entendre* – than either of us reckoned on.

The sergeant dropped the match and looked at his watch – in the dark.

"Dear me!" he exclaimed. "I mustn't stay loitering here, fascinating as these antiquities are. I shall lose my train."

"Your train!" I exclaimed.

"Yes. I've got to run up to Chatham. Nuisance, isn't it?"

I wasn't so sure of that, but, of course, I agreed that it was; and when we had each contributed a practically unearned increment to the sexton's income, we ascended the steps and made our way out through the churchyard.

"Awful nuisance," repeated Burbler. "I shall probably be detained in Chatham for two or three days. Most annoying! Just as I was enjoying me holiday, too!"

"I thought you were down here on business."

"So I was. But my business is finished. Another officer has taken over the case" – and no wonder, thought I – "so I am having a little rest; taking a week or two's leave. They might have left me in peace."

Now here I was seized by an absurd and reprehensible impulse to say what was not strictly true. The sergeant was going away. While

unavoidably absent he might be uneasy in his mind. He might even
return prematurely. It would be only humane to reassure him.

"I can sympathize with you," I prevaricated, "for I'm in the same
boat myself."

The pleasure that shone from Burbler's face seemed almost to
justify me.

"Not going away?" he said brightly.

"Yes. Got to go to – er – Tunbridge Wells for my firm. They may
keep me there a week or so. Nuisance for me, isn't it?"

"Horrid," said Burbler. "Do you start today?"

Of course, I had to say "yes", and the detective immediately
pounced on me.

"What time is your train?"

Now there he had me, for I had neglected to ask the time of his.
In my confusion I said "four o'clock", and he chimed in gleefully:

"I know. Four-eight. Change at Tonbridge. Mine is the four-fifty
from the other station. I may as well walk down with you and see you
off."

Thus was I hoist with my own petard. For I had meant to see him
off and then prepare at my leisure for a nocturnal exploration of the
crypt. But there was no escape. I was led like a sacrificial lamb to the
station and compelled, under the sergeant's scrutiny, to waste my substance on a ticket for Tunbridge Wells. Indeed, fate, in the form of
Sergeant Burbler, pursued me to the very door of the compartment
in which I didn't want to travel.

"Look out!" he exclaimed. "The train's off!" And whisking open a
door, he gave me a persuasive hoist that deposited me on the lap of a
fierce-looking, middle-aged woman.

"How dare you, sir?" demanded the lady, assisting me to rise with
the aid of an extraordinarily sharp elbow. "What do you mean by this
conduct?"

"I beg your pardon, Madam," I gasped, retreating to the farthest
corner. "It was purely an accident, I assure you. It was indeed!"

"I don't know what you mean by an accident," she rejoined bitterly; "bursting into a compartment that is plainly labelled 'Ladies only'. It is an unwarrantable intrusion!"

I glanced at the window and saw that it was even as she had said. However, it didn't matter. I was going to pop out at the next station, Chartham, in any case, and make my way back to Canterbury. I mentioned the fact in extenuation.

"Chartham indeed!" she replied scornfully. "Permit me to remark that this train does not stop until it reaches Tonbridge."

I was aghast. Here was a pretty kettle of fish! I should have to buy another useless ticket and put off my exploration until tomorrow; for the shops would all be shut when I got back to Canterbury, and I couldn't lift that stone with my fingernails. Of course I could carry out my little plan just as well tomorrow night – unless Burbler should return prematurely. And here I broke out into a cold sweat; for nothing was more likely. He had located the treasure and he knew that I had, too. He was certain to strain every nerve to get back and forestall me. It was a horrible predicament.

What made it worse was that my efforts to think out some escape from the situation were completely frustrated by my fellow passenger; who continued to pour out an unceasing stream of reproaches for my "unwarrantable intrusion". How she did talk, to be sure! If some of those perpetual motion chappies could have examined that good woman's lower jaw, they might have got a valuable tip or two. The usual metaphor of the donkey's hind leg was inadequate; she would have talked the fifty hind legs off a centipede.

The train whizzed joyfully through station after station. It roared through Ashford and left Pluckley behind, trundled along the straight stretch towards Paddock Wood and Tonbridge. But presently it began to slow down and at length came definitely to a stop at the little wayside halt of Helgerden.

"Now, sir," said my companion, "I'll trouble you to change into another compartment."

I hesitated; for the train was only waiting for the signal to drop and might move on at any moment. But eventually I was goaded into opening the door and stepping out.

"Hi, sir! you can't get out here!" exclaimed the stationmaster, regardless of the fact that I had actually done so. And at this moment the train began to move. I made a dash for the nearest door, but the stationmaster seized me by the arm.

"You can't enter the train when in motion," he said obscurely; and before I could wriggle myself free, the guard had hopped in and the train had rumbled out of the station.

"What time is the next train to Canterbury?" I asked.

"Ten-forty," he replied, and added: "I must ask you, sir, not to use such language before my porter."

I apologized and pleaded extreme provocation, explaining that I had got into the wrong train and wished to get back quickly.

"Well, sir," he said, "there's a very good train from Ashford in about an hour's time."

"And how long will it take me to walk into Ashford?"

"If you step out, sir," he replied, "you ought to do it in an hour and three-quarters."

I turned away hastily – appropriate remarks being forbidden – and, striding wrathfully out of the station, walked through the village until I encountered a finger-post which bore the inscription: "Ashford 7½ miles." Along this road I set forth at a brisk pace: but before I had gone two hundred yards I found myself face to face with a most terrible temptation. Leaning against a barn was an abandoned bicycle; a tradesman's machine apparently, for on the top bar was painted the name "Robert Miker". Now, with that bicycle I could easily catch the desirable train from Ashford. Without it I must walk and my operations in the crypt would have to be postponed – perhaps for ever. The catching or losing of that train might spell the difference between gaining and losing a fortune.

I say nothing in extenuation of my conduct. Property should not be borrowed without the consent of the owner. But – there was no one about from whom to ask permission. I flung my leg over the saddle and away I went.

I have said that when I mounted there was not a soul to be seen. But before I had fairly got the wheels revolving, the entire population of the place seemed to converge on the spot to speed my departure with valedictory hoots. A shrill voice commanded me to "come off that bike" and a deeper voice hailed me to stop. Looking back, I saw (among others) a weedy youth shaking his fist in my direction and a globular-bodied rural constable coming after me at a speed that was really amazing when one considered his proportions. I had heard of the agility of the rhinoceros but I had never believed in it until I saw that rural constable. Still, he was no match for a cyclist.

When I next looked round, a light carrier's cart had appeared. It soon became less light, for the constable got in; and then the driver plied his whip and the cart came along in my wake, clattering like the horses and chariots in Pharaoh's pursuing army. I pedalled for all I was worth. It was too late to change my mind now. And though that cart hung on doggedly, it grew smaller and smaller in the increasing distance. The last that I saw of it was at a crossroad, down which it turned, leaving the constable a tiny, threatening spot on the white highway.

A little way past the milestone that recorded "three miles to Ashford", I came to a small inn which bore on its signboard the words "White Cow". I had now plenty of time in which to walk the rest of the way, and it seemed a wise thing to disencumber myself of my borrowed steed. Entering, I ordered a glass of beer, and, having hastily consumed it, I asked the landlord to take charge of the bicycle.

"It belongs to Mr Miker," I explained. "I expect he will call for it by and by. Will you give it to him and tell him that I am much obliged for the loan of it?"

The landlord promised to give the message, and I then got on the road once more, stepping out at a good round pace and congratulating myself on having made a skilful escape from a compromising situation. Soon after leaving the inn I came to a rather steep hill, at the top of which the road ran along the level for some considerable distance before again descending. I had proceeded along the level tract and was close to the brow of the hill when I became aware of the hum of a bicycle, approaching rapidly from behind. I looked quickly over my shoulder, and my heart sank. Ye Gods and little fishes! It was that confounded rural constable!

I gave one despairing glance at the town of Ashford, spread out before my yearning gaze. Another couple of miles and I had been safe. It was a pitiful thing to be shipwrecked within sight of port, but shipwrecked I apparently was. For the constable swept alongside, and dismounting lightly, laid a colossal paw on my shoulder.

"Got yer!" said he.

I turned sharply, and casting on him a disdainful glance, demanded haughtily:

"What the deuce do you mean?"

"You know what I mean," he replied. "I charge you with stealing this bicycle."

I laughed scornfully; though I didn't feel much like laughing, I can assure you.

"My good man," said I, "how on earth can I have stolen the bicycle when you have got it in your possession?"

"Now don't argue with me," he retorted. "I've caught you in *flagranto delictum*. Saw yer prig it with my own eyes. You just come along back with me."

It was a desperate situation and called for desperate efforts. I thought frantically for a few seconds and then burst into a hollow laugh, pointing at the bicycle.

"Why," I exclaimed, "that's the machine that I left at the 'White Cow'!"

"Quite right," said the constable.

"Ha! ha!" I shouted. "You are actually charging me with stealing my own bicycle on which my name is legibly painted for all the world to see. Look here!" and I pointed to the inscription.

The constable began to look puzzled. "Your name ain't Robert Miker," said he. "This here bike belongs to young Bob Miker, the wheelwright."

"Oh, I see," said I. "You are confusing me with some other Robert Miker. How very amusing! Most ridiculous comedy of errors! But I'll soon prove to you that this is my bicycle. You noticed that peculiar tilt of the right pedal?"

"No, I didn't," he replied.

"Didn't you really?" said I, cocking up my right great toe. "I'm surprised at that. I had the pedal specially built to fit this slight deformity of my right foot."

The constable stared at the pedal and then at my foot, which certainly had a rather quaint appearance with the toe cocking up inside the boot.

"I don't see nothing peculiar about the pedal," said he.

"Let me show you," said I. "You'll see at once if I place my foot on the pedal. It twists up on the inside. You'll see it better if you stoop a little. Now."

I placed my foot on the pedal and he crouched down in the attitude of a frog preparing to spring, his mouth open and his eyes protruding with intelligent curiosity.

"Don't you see?" I asked.

"No, I don't," he replied.

I gave his shoulder a sharp push: and, as he toppled over backwards like an overturned china mandarin, making a frantic snatch at me as he fell, I stood up on the pedal and flung my left leg over the saddle. The bicycle started forward and I urged it with all my strength. But it was a near thing. The constable picked himself up in a moment and came bouncing along the road like a gigantic football. Indeed, if it had not been for the sharp descent he would have caught me before the machine had time to get up speed. As it was, I went over the brow of the hill and picked up speed in two or three revolutions. And then, of course, the constable was nowhere. In a few seconds I was flying down the hill at twenty or thirty miles an hour, and even when I reached the level at the bottom, I kept up the pace so far as I was able until I ran into the station approach at Ashford.

I had just time to take my ticket and book the bicycle (in the name of Miker) before the train rumbled into the station. Selecting an empty carriage, I took a corner seat by the door and, flinging my hat into the rack, wiped my brow. For the moment, I was safe. I had run the two miles in about seven minutes and the constable couldn't do it in much under half an hour. But he would get to the station before I should reach Canterbury, and he would probably telegraph my description. That was awkward. And the train did not stop at any intermediate station. It was very awkward.

The bell rang; a smartly-dressed Hebrew gentleman in a new straw hat bustled into my compartment, and the train started. I resumed my disquieting reflections. Could a telegraphed description lead to identification? I doubted it. I wore a common tweed suit and so did most of the other men in the train. I was dark, with aquiline features; but so were plenty of other men. The only distinctive feature in my get-up was my hat – a green soft felt. That hat was the weak spot in my armour. I hadn't noticed another like it on the platform. If I had been alone I would have dropped it out of the window and risked going through the barrier hatless; but there was the Hebrew chappie opposite. He would see me drop it and might give information.

I had not solved the problem when the train ran into Canterbury. My fellow passenger stood up and thrust his head and shoulders out of the window. I stood up, too – and – quite automatically, as it seemed – reached the Hebrew gentleman's straw hat down from the rack and clapped it on my head. It was a loosish fit, but that didn't matter. Then my companion popped his head in and asked me:

"Do I change here for Margate?"

Now the fact is that he should have changed, but – well, necessity knows no law.

"No," I replied. "Stay where you are," and with this I hopped out and walked quickly through the barrier. By the side of the ticket collector I noticed a tall, burly man who seemed to eye the passengers curiously, but he was no concern of mine. I hurried through and made for the exit. But just as I was passing out, I heard a loud commotion from the neighbourhood of the barrier. I cast an instantaneous glance back and saw that tall, burly man struggling with a Hebrew gentleman in a green felt hat. And I waited to see no more.

The shops were still open when I emerged from the station and dived down the first by-street. I zigzagged through quiet lanes and courts to the farther side of the town – dropping the cloakroom ticket into a convenient letter box on my way – and, having bought a cloth cap and deposited the straw hat (which was marked inside "I Cohen") in a deep doorway in an unfrequented by-street, I began to consider the outfit necessary for my proposed raid on Simon Glynn's vault. A crowbar, a pick and a shovel were what was really needed; but this equipment would be just a trifle conspicuous. Besides, I really did not contemplate operations on that scale. If there was actual digging to be done, I should have to compound with Burbler and share the proceeds. The outfit that I eventually purchased at the tool shop consisted of a large case-opener – practically a small crowbar – a half-dozen window wedges (to prevent the stone from dropping back when I had prised it up), one or two candles, and a botanist's trowel; a feeble set of appliances, but sufficient if it was only a question of lifting a covering stone and exploring a vault.

"The shades of night were falling fast" when I approached the village of Bouldersby by a solitary footpath. I had not hurried; for time was no object. And I was not hurrying now. On the contrary, I found my footsteps lagging more and more as the distance lessened and the old church loomed up more distinctly in the gathering gloom. It was not mere caution that made me linger, though I went mighty warily and kept a bright lookout. The fact is, that as I drew nearer to the church, I began to develop a most uncommon distaste for the job. It is all very well to sneer at vulgar superstition, but there is something very revolting in the idea of breaking into the resting place of the dead in the mere, sordid search for money. Moreover, it was only now that I began fully to realize the extreme vagueness of my quest. Supposing I got the vault open? What then? The treasure could not be exposed to view, or the people who buried Simon, himself, would have seen it. And if it was hidden in the vault, what clue had I to the hiding place?

It was quite dark when, in a chastened, and even depressed, frame of mind, I sneaked in through the lychgate and crept stealthily across the churchyard. Through the open and lighted windows of the adjoining rectory there stole out into the summer night sounds of revelry and mirth, including a mid-Victorian solo by a brassy-voiced gentleman who (according to his own statement) bore the unusual name of "Champagne Charley". The light and life, the laughter and the gay, if unmelodious song, seemed by contrast to accentuate the sordid gruesomeness of my ghoulish quest. Tremulously and guiltily I sought the little doorway and groped my way down the mossy steps, not daring to strike a light for fear of being seen from the rectory windows.

The crypt was as dark as a vault. I had to back down the last few steps on all fours, and, when I reached the bottom, I felt my way along the wall to the farthest corner. And here I thought it safe to strike a match and light one of my candles.

But I was loath to begin. I unpacked my parcel of tools and laid them on the stone floor, speculating once more on what I should do when I got down into the vault. Then I examined the joints of the stone that I was to raise and was almost disappointed to find them amply wide enough to admit the chisel-edge of the case-opener. At last, violently screwing up my courage to the sticking point, I seized the case-opener and one or two wedges and prepared to make the first, repulsive effort. And at that moment my ear caught distinctly a sound of movement from somewhere above with an audible metallic clink.

Instantly, I blew out my candle, and, standing stock-still, listened. The sounds were repeated − nearer, this time: and then I heard a fumbling footstep on the stone stairs and again the clink of metal. I shrank back into the uttermost corner; a useless proceeding, for there was not cover enough to conceal an earwig. The intruder reached the floor, and, having laid on it some metallic objects, struck a match, by the light of which I saw a large man with his back towards me. He was lighting a sort of Guy Fawkes lantern such as carters use, and, when he had got the wick alight, he turned towards me, staring into the lantern as he regulated the flame, so that the light shone full on his face. Need I say that the face was that of Sergeant Burbler?

Having adjusted the wick, the detective threw the light of the lantern round the crypt and, naturally, its rays fell upon me; whereupon the sergeant opened his eyes and mouth unnecessarily widely and let fall one or two unconsidered remarks which I need not report *verbatim*.

"I thought you were at Tunbridge Wells, Mr Cobb!" he concluded.

"I thought you were at Chatham!" I retorted.

"Well, I came back unexpectedly," said he.

"So did I," was my rejoinder.

An embarrassing silence followed during which we eyed one another with hostile stares. Finally the sergeant's face relaxed into a sour grin.

"Well, here we are," said he, stating an incontestable truth. "It's no good gaping at one another like a couple of fools. I suppose it will have to be a partnership job. That suit you?"

"Perfectly," I replied. "We go halves, of course?"

"That's it. And, look here, Mr Cobb: we keep our mouths shut about this little affair. This is a matter of treasure trove, and I suppose you know how the law stands, being, I understand, a sort of half-baked lawyer."

"Nothing of the kind, sir!" I exclaimed indignantly. "I am an articled clerk and I shall be a fully qualified solicitor in a few months. And I may tell you that this is not a case of treasure-trove. We are acting on the express instructions of the deceased. I regard that inscription on the mirror as having a testamentary character. The treasure is definitely stated to be a personal bequest to the finder."

"I doubt if a court of law would take that view," said Burbler. "Anyhow, it will be safer for us to keep our own counsel. Morally speaking, the stuff is ours, and that is all that matters."

This being an eminently reasonable view to take of the case, I agreed to inviolable secrecy as to the treasure, and the sergeant then began his preparations. His outfit was a much more businesslike one than mine, for it included a small spade and a very large and massive folding jemmy. The latter, when the joints were screwed together, was about three feet long and was a decidedly hefty tool for use either as a crow or a pick; and when the sergeant had "jumped" its beak into the joint between the stones, one or two vigorous heaves at the knobbed handle fairly lifted the inscribed slab out of its bed.

"Now, Mr Cobb," exclaimed Burbler, "just stick that bar of yours into the opening while I get a fresh purchase."

I thrust in the case-opener, and the sergeant took a fresh purchase with his jemmy. Another strong heave, and the stone came up a couple of inches. I seized its edge and held it until the sergeant, dropping the jemmy, came to my assistance. Then with a united effort we hoisted the stone right up and turned it back, disclosing a square, black hole and the top of a flight of brick steps.

It was an uninviting-looking entrance and we both gazed at it in silence and without any enthusiastic tendency to struggle for precedence.

"Well," the sergeant remarked, at length, "it's a small hole, Mr Cobb; we can't both go down at once."

I admitted that we could not, and suggested the propriety of lowering the lantern to make sure that the air was not too foul.

"Yes, that's true," said Burbler, "but I haven't got any string. Just hold the lantern down at arm's length and see how it burns."

I lay down on the pavement and let the lantern down as far as I could reach. It burned quite well but failed to make the interior of the vault clearly visible; in fact, I could see nothing at all save an enormous cluster of horrible-looking fungi which occupied the lower steps and generated in me an urgent desire to see Burbler go down first.

I lifted up the lantern, and the sergeant and I gazed at one another irresolutely. And then the deathly silence of the crypt was suddenly shattered by a brassy voice which shouted:

"Body-snatchers, by jingo!"

The sergeant and I leaped to our feet, and Burbler nearly fell down the hole. The light of the lantern revealed two men, one of whom – a fiddle-faced, red-jowled old sinner who looked like a retired military officer – was in evening dress, while the other was obviously a clergyman. The newcomers stared at us and we stared at them; and a very embarrassing situation it was for the sergeant and me.

"Taken red-handed, by Jove!" said the violin-faced warrior. "Caught on the bally hop! What!"

As this remark, though vulgarly expressed, stated an undeniable truth, no comment seemed to be called for. Moreover, neither the sergeant nor I was at the moment bursting with conversational matter. So we continued to gape at the intruders like a couple of fools.

Then the parson spoke.

"Would you kindly explain," said he, "what is the meaning of these very strange proceedings?"

I left the explanation to Burbler as the more expert and accomplished liar. But he was not so ready as I should have expected. He gibbered confusedly for a few seconds and then replied with a most unconvincing stammer:

"We are −er− engaged in −er−er− archæological research."

The parson smiled faintly and the warrior, glaring ferociously at Burbler, growled:

"Archæological bunkum!" and then fixed an inquisitive eye on the sergeant's jemmy.

"If you wish to know what is under this crypt," said the parson," I can save you the trouble of further excavation, for I was not only present but I personally supervised the reconstruction of the Glynn vault some twenty years ago."

"Indeed!" gasped Burbler.

"Yes. There seems to have been some silly tradition of a buried treasure in the vault, and as a result we suffered a good deal of inconvenience. There was a tendency on the part of unauthorized persons to injure the iron gate and − and, in short, to engage in archæological research."

Here the fiddle-faced ass flung up his fat head and roared:

"Ha! ha! Archæological, by gum! Dam good that! Excuse me, Padre."

"So," pursued the parson, "I thought it desirable to set the matter at rest by a thorough examination of the vault. Needless to say, nothing was discovered beyond the bones of the deceased and the decayed remnants of two oaken coffins. I had the entire floor of the crypt dug up and the foundations examined, and then the vault was rebuilt, the remains re-coffined, and the pavement of the crypt relaid as you see it now. Is there anything else that you would like to know?"

"No, thank you," replied Burbler. "That settles our hash – I mean to say, that is all the information that we require."

"Then, in that case, perhaps you would like me to show you the most convenient way out of the precincts?"

"Thank you, it's very good of you, sir," said Burbler: and the parson rejoined: "Not at all."

We picked up our ridiculous tools – excepting the jemmy, which the warrior pounced on and examined attentively before handing it to the sergeant – and took our way sadly up the steps and along the churchyard path. At the lychgate the parson wished us a courteous "Good evening", and his companion leaned over the gate and bellowed after us:

"You've had a devilish easy let-off, you two rascals. Suppose you know it's a misdemeanour to be found at night with housebreaking tools? What? Oh, I know a jemmy when I see one, don't you make any mistake!"

"I expect you do," snapped Burbler. "Done a bit in that line yourself, eh?" and he turned away, leaving the fiddle-faced warrior gasping.

The sergeant and I trudged dejectedly along the high road, and for a while neither of us spoke. At length I ventured to remark:

"Well, sergeant, Simon Glynn has been one too many for us this time."

But Burbler's heart was too full for conversation. He only replied with a morose growl:

"Damn Simon Glynn."

CHAPTER FIVE

A Mermaid and a Red Herring

There is a world of difference as to the resulting knowledge between a cursory observation that notes only generalities and an attentive examination that considers particular details. I realized this with great force when, having strolled out from my lodgings at the Royal George inn to smoke my morning pipe on the little green, I turned to look up at the picturesque house. Between the middle windows, close under the eaves, was a small square of stone in which were cut three initial letters and a date. I had noticed it when I first came to the inn and I had frequently glanced at it since; but if I had been asked to describe the inscription I could have told no more than that it consisted of three initial letters surrounding a heart with the date 1636 underneath. What the letters were I certainly could not have told, though I should have remembered the date.

The explanation of this is perfectly simple. A group of figures forming a date conveys a definite meaning, whereas the initial letters of an unknown person's name have none; and meaningless things neither stimulate the attention nor impress the memory.

Yet I had often looked, and not without interest, at the little tablet. For these simple memorials illustrate a very pretty old-world custom. The initials – usually set in a triangle about a heart or flower or star – are those of a man and wife and the date below is that on which the house was finished and the young couple entered into possession to begin their married life. The upper letter is the initial of the joint surname and the lower ones represent the Christian names of the husband and wife respectively.

This morning I was in a reflective vein and somewhat at a loose end. Only the previous day I had made that abortive search in the vault. The treasure, deliberately hidden by old Simon over two centuries ago, was still undiscovered. I had been hot on the scent; and though that scent had proved a false one, the search had warmed my blood with the treasure-hunting fever.

I looked up at the tablet and somewhat absently read the brief inscription. The upper letter was G; the lower two S and M. And then I started, suddenly wide awake. For these were the initials of Simon and Margery Glynn.

At first I thought it must be a mere coincidence. Glynn was a man of means who lived in the great house of Elham Manor. How should his name appear on this obscure wayside inn? The initials must be those of some other couple; Solomon and Miriam Gobbler, for instance. But then there was the date, 1636. I made a rapid calculation from the dates on Glynn's tomb in Bouldersby church. He died in 1692, aged eighty-one. Then in 1636 he was twenty-five years old; a very likely age at which to marry and settle down. Margery Glynn died in 1662, aged forty-five. Then in 1636 she would be nineteen; again a very likely age. It looked uncommonly as if these initials were those of Glynn and his wife.

Suddenly I recalled a passage in Boteler's "Manor Houses of Kent", which stated that "from a reference to him (Glynn) in Pepys' Diary, it would seem that he had property in this neighbourhood, of which he was probably a native". Now it happened that, only a day or two previously, I had picked up on a bookstall in Canterbury an old copy of Pepys' Diary, which I had not looked at since. Full of my new discovery, I bustled indoors, and, running up to my room, opened the volume and eagerly ran my eye down the index, until it lighted on the name "Glynn, Simon", when, with a trembling hand, I turned up the entry.

"23rd April (1664). Upp and to the Coffee House by the Exchange to talk with Mr Gannett a Turky Merchant. While we are talking comes Mr Simon Glynn (a Goldsmith and Secretary of the Mint in Oliver's time) a pleasant fellow but whimsicall. Much good discourse and merriment. Mr Gannett asketh Glynn how he, being a widower without issue, shall devise his wealth; to which Glynn answers that his house and lands and a tavern that he hath he shall give to his sister's sons, but not his money. And then he makes this observation (which methought mighty pretty) viz:– That some doe possess much money and little wit, and others much wit and little money, but whoso inherits his gatherings shall have both."

Here was matter indeed! There could be very little doubt that the "tavern that he hath" was the very inn in which I was lodging; and that concluding observation seemed to hint that when Simon deposited his "gatherings" in a hiding place for the benefit of some future treasure-hunter, he intended that "wit" and not chance should be the instrument of its discovery. And no doubt he had made suitable arrangements. At any rate, upwards of two centuries had passed, and, though, according to all accounts, there had been no lack of treasure-seekers, Simon Glynn's hoard still waited for the adventurer with wit enough to locate it.

Was it possible that I was to be that fortunate adventurer? Elham Manor house had been ransacked again and again, its garden excavated and its very panelling torn down; the vault under the church had been opened and dug out to the foundations. But no one, so far as I knew, had ever searched the tavern; indeed, its connection with Glynn would appear to have been forgotten. Which might easily have happened, seeing that the existence of hidden treasure did not become known until nearly half a century after Simon's death.

Since the finding of the mirror every likely place seemed to have been searched. The Manor House had been searched; the vault under the monument had been explored. But no treasure had come to light. The treasure-seekers had apparently struck the wrong place each time.

Could it be that Glynn had after all secreted his savings somewhere in the inn? It was intrinsically probable enough. The small house in which he had made his start in life and to which he had brought home his young wife, must have had happier memories for him than the stately Manor House in which he had lived a solitary widower. It was highly probable that he would choose that place in which to hide his curious legacy; but – there was not the slightest evidence that he had. No vestige of any harp or cross or anchors three had I seen since I had lodged at the inn.

But wait! There was one thing that I had seen and had meant to investigate. On the main gable of the house – which, oddly enough, looked on the garden and the river – was some kind of tablet or ornamental panel of carved brick. Only a corner of the moulding that framed it was visible, the whole of the remainder being hidden by a too-luxuriant creeper; but the size of the frame showed that it was a work of more pretensions than the little tablet on the front of the house.

I walked through into the garden, and, backing away from the house until I was stopped by the great mulberry tree that dominated the lawn, looked up at the gable. The corner of a well-carved frame poked out from under the creeper; and, even as I looked, a breath of wind lifted the foliage and showed me the date 1640. That settled it. The panel was put up in Glynn's time. The frame almost certainly enclosed some kind of sculpture. Perhaps a harp and a cross – but I would soon see. For my bedroom window was just underneath it and the principal branch of the offending creeper was within easy reach.

Full of my investigation and oblivious of the remoter consequences of what I was about to do, I ran up to my bedroom and thrust my head out of the window. The panel was but a few feet above, embedded in the mass of creeper that covered the gable. I grasped the large branch that strayed past the jamb of the window and gave it a gentle pull. The plant was a species of Virginia creeper; the kind which attaches itself to the wall without artificial support, though not with the security of the less handsome ampelopsis; and, as I pulled, I could feel some of the little tendrils break away. I gave one or two more jerks – quite gentle ones lest I should damage the possibly fragile ornament of the panel. At each jerk I felt more of the tendrils break and then suddenly the whole branch separated from the wall and came tumbling down so that I had to cut it through with my knife and let it drop to the ground.

Once more I thrust out my head and looked up; but crane out as I might, I could see no more than the bottom edge of the frame, though the gable was now clear of the creeper. But if I could not see the panel, there was somebody else who could. I observed him just as I was withdrawing my head, and in a moment realized what an idiot I had been. The man was standing under a clump of willows on the opposite side of the river and was in such deep shadow that I could not see what he was like, though it was clear enough that he was looking up at the gable and mightily interested in my proceedings. But though I could not recognize him, an uneasy suspicion as to his identity flitted through my mind; a suspicion that this untimely observer was none other than Detective-Sergeant Burbler.

If this should really turn out to be the case, then I had brought my pigs to a pretty fine market! For the worthy detective, who had come down to this neighbourhood on official business, was admittedly staying here for his own purposes. He was "taking a few weeks' leave to enjoy the quiet and the beautiful scenery". That was how he put it. The actual fact was that he had caught the scent of Simon Glynn's treasure and was hanging about in the hope of picking up some further clues. And, as he believed me to be in possession of some private information respecting the hiding place of that treasure, he had made it his special business to shadow me ever since I had begun my researches. He hadn't got much by his shadowing up to the present, for the simple reason that there had been nothing to get. I knew no more than he. But now, by uncovering that panel for all the world to see, I had, perhaps, put him in possession of a valuable clue.

I raced down the stairs, all agog to see what that panel really was. Hurrying out into the garden, I backed away under the great mulberry tree and looked up. And as my eye lighted on the carved brick sculpture enclosed within the frame, a wave of mingled exultation and alarm swept over me; exultation because here was a first-class clue; alarm lest my inveterate rival should have seen it too.

For the panel exhibited in bold relief the figure of an unmistakable mermaid.

It was clearly not the work of an ordinary village mason. The ornament of the frame was but a plain and simple lattice pattern, but the figure was quite competently done; entirely unlike the crude and childish figure-work of the rustic sculptor. Indeed, the whole panel, in both design and finish, was singularly out of character with the homely building – little more than a cottage – on which it was placed; and this suggested that by the year 1640 Glynn had already begun to be a prosperous man. Probably he worked here at his trade, while his wife managed the inn, and found in the city hard by plenty of customers for his work.

But the immediate question was as to the meaning of this sculptured figure. I repeated the doggerel lines:

"Ankores three atte the foot of a tree and a maid from the sea on high."

And it was instantly borne in on me that I was standing at the foot of a tree to look up at the sea-maid; and that, as there was no other tree near, this was the only one that could possibly be referred to. I turned to look at the mulberry tree. Obviously, it was of great age. It might well have been – and probably was – planted by Glynn himself. And if it was; if Glynn had planted it soon after he came to the house in 1636, then, at the time when the treasure was buried – which was, apparently, about 1684 – it would be nearly fifty years old and quite a large and well-grown tree. The reasonable inference was that this was the tree referred to in the doggerel and that Simon Glynn's hoard was buried at its foot.

Of course there were objections to this conclusion. There was no sign of any harp or cross and the "ankores three" were nowhere to be seen. But the harp and cross might easily have been removed by Vandalic "restorers" if they were originally carved on, or affixed to, the house; and as to the anchors, they were probably incised on the bark of the tree itself, and, if so, would naturally have disappeared after all these years. Simon Glynn could never have reckoned that two hundred and thirty years would elapse before a really intelligent man should appear to claim his legacy. It was unsatisfactory, I could not but admit, that those confirmatory signs were absent; but still, there was the tree, and there was the "maid from the sea on high", and that seemed good enough to justify a careful exploration.

Already a delighted imagination was filling in the outline of the picture. I saw the hole at the foot of the mulberry tree and heard the thud as my pick or spade impinged on the iron-bound chest: and I was beginning to speculate on the nature of the precious contents, when, suddenly, the recollection of Burbler came like the shadow of the Upas Tree, to blot out the sunlight of my dreams. Had he seen me uncover the panel? or was that figure under the willows merely a chance rustic, curious but innocuous?

I ran down to the landing stage and, getting into the boat that belonged to the inn, pulled upstream. But there was no one under the willows now. I landed and searched the neighbourhood of the towpath, but not a soul was to be seen. Rustic loiterer or watchful detective, that unwelcome observer had vanished and left no trace.

With mixed feelings, in which pleasurable excitement predominated, I pulled back to the inn and landed. The suspicion that Burbler had seen the tell-tale figure of the mermaid could not influence my course of action except to hasten it. At the foot of the mulberry tree lay Simon Glynn's "gatherings". Of that I had very little doubt. The course was to dig them up; and, under the circumstances, the sooner the better. I had the great advantage over Burbler that I was a resident of the inn. When the premises were shut up for the night I should have the place practically to myself, for old Mrs Hodger, my landlady, was the only other person who slept in the house, and she was as deaf as a post. When once she had retired to her room in the front of the house, which she usually did about ten o'clock, I was as free as if I were quite alone.

The necessary preparations were few and simple and I had the day before me in which to make them. First I visited the cellar, in which I knew the garden tools were kept. There was a good enough assortment; two spades and three stout forks, in addition to the smaller tools. Unfortunately, however, there was no pick. But to dig a deep hole in undisturbed ground without a pick was a task that I felt to be beyond me; and accordingly I set forth, without delay, to procure the necessary implement from a tool shop in Canterbury. I kept a sharp lookout for Burbler, whose unpleasant habit of shadowing and spying on me I have mentioned, and when I emerged from the shop with the pick, thinly disguised in brown paper, I made at once for the least frequented by-streets and left the town by a footpath across the meadows. But it was an anxious business; for if the detective had met me with that incriminating tool under my arm, the murder would have been out with a vengeance. I should never have got a chance to use it.

But it seemed that I was in luck, for the perilous passage was accomplished without my seeing any sign of Burbler. I sneaked into the inn by the garden door and at once proceeded to deposit the pick in a corner of the cellar. So far, good. I had made my preparations unobserved. If I had the same luck with my midnight explorations, I might get the treasure safely stowed in my trunk before Burbler was ready to begin. That is, assuming that my worst suspicions of him were correct.

In this mood of self-congratulation I slowly ascended the cellar steps. But at the top I halted and my self-congratulations came to a sudden end. In fact, I got a most severe shock.

A deaf person somewhat resembles a telephone; which appears to be an appliance for conveying verbal information to everybody but the person addressed. There was a stranger in the bar. I knew he was a stranger because he was talking to Mrs Hodger. The regular customers simply reached down a mug from the shelf and held it under the tap of the selected cask. But what had filled me with consternation was the sound of the voice. It was pitched in a low and confidential key, and the words were indistinguishable but I seemed to recognize it.

"Ah," said Mrs Hodger, "you're right. This hot weather do make you thirsty. So much the better for me. He! he!"

The stranger rejoined, a little louder; and, though I could not hear what he said, I knew that he was repeating his former remark. Strangers always did.

"Well," said Mrs Hodger, "what I says is, wooden taps is better'n lead pipes when all's said 'n done. More wholesome, like, you know."

Here the stranger, abandoning his former confidential and rather secret tone, let off a howl that must have been audible half a mile away. And that howl settled the question of the speaker's identity.

"I'm – asking – you," roared the unmistakable voice of Sergeant Burbler, "if you can – let – me – have – a Bedroom?"

Mrs Hodger evidently had some slight misgivings as to whether she had quite caught that last remark. But she was a woman of spirit.

"Ho," she replied, "then you'd better get a mug down and droar it yourself. Then you'll know that you've got what you want."

There was a short pause. I knew what was coming; and it came, sure enough. It always did.

"There ain't any need to write it," said Mrs Hodger, a little huffily. "I may be a trifle hard of hearing, but this ain't an asylum for the deaf and dumb... Oh, I see. Got a sore throat and lost your voice? Dear, dear. Surprising what a lot o' people is took that way nowadays. There's my lodger, Mr Cobb, and the Rector and – but you're asking about a bedroom. Well, you can have the little blue room if you'll take things as they come and not expect no waiting on."

Apparently the little blue room – so called from the colour of its paint – answered Burbler's requirements, for he turned up that very day about teatime accompanied by a barrow on which was a large cabin trunk and an elongated parcel enclosed in sacking. That parcel looked as if it contained a spade and pick, but I couldn't be quite sure, as Burbler declined my offer to carry it upstairs for him.

Now here was a nice cheerful state of affairs! Of course, my proposed nocturnal exploration was impossible so long as Burbler was about. And he seemed to have come to stay. At any rate he would probably see my visit out, for I couldn't squeeze more than a week or two of extended holiday out of my firm, indulgent as they were.

It was an intolerable situation. Burbler clung to me as if I had been a long-lost brother. He walked abroad with me, of course he took meals with me, and he would even pop into my bedroom unexpectedly when I was dressing – though I put a stopper on that by bolting the door. Even when I escaped for a few minutes' quiet, I have reason to believe that he consoled himself by visiting my room and raking over my personal effects; an intrusion that I was powerless to prevent, for, though every door in the house seemed to be fitted with massive bolts inside and out, there was not a single workable lock.

It is true that Burbler's conduct was not without its compensations; for if he could not afford to lose sight of me, neither could I afford to lose sight of him. And there was a further consolation. The continual watch that he kept over my movements and especially his repeated searchings in my room showed that he still believed me to possess some clue to the whereabouts of the treasure that he did not. Still, as I have said, it was an intolerable situation and something would have to be done. There, I felt no doubt, was the treasure, lying *perdu* at the foot of the mulberry tree, and, somehow, by hook or by crook, I must manage to get it exhumed.

Necessity is the mother of invention. During those dreary walks with Burbler my brain was hard at work; while I sat at table with him I turned over scheme after scheme; and especially in the watches of the night, when I lay by the open window listening for the sound of a surreptitious pick from the lawn below, was my mind busy with plans for getting rid of Burbler. And at last I hit on one.

It was clear to me that the sergeant did not share my certainty as to where the treasure was hidden. Not being gifted, like me, with a brilliant constructive imagination, he was baffled by the absence of the Harp, the Cross and the "Ankores three". Hence his continual attendance on me and his searchings of my room. He thought I knew more than he did, and he was waiting for me to give him a lead. Very well. I would give him one.

The inspiration of my plan came from a prehistoric monument that stood in a field not far from the inn; a structure of the kind known as a dolmen – a sort of rude tomb chamber roofed in by a huge, flat "table-stone". Near to it was the hollow trunk of an ancient oak, which, with it, occupied a space that was reserved from cultivation. There is something rather stimulating to the imagination in these prehistoric remains, especially when associated with an ancient and decayed oak. Not that Burbler had much imagination; but it was as well to give him all the assistance possible.

I made a preliminary sketch plan of the place and then, after breakfast, while Burbler was giving his boots a brush in the scullery, I sneaked out of the house and legged it as hard as I could go. The dolmen was visible from the road across one or two open meadows, and I suspected that I shouldn't have it very long to myself. Nor had I. Within five minutes of my arrival a distant figure appeared getting over a fence and approaching; somewhat circuitously, it is true, for the adjoining meadow, through which the direct footpath led, was occupied by Farmer Babbage's short-horn bull. I affected not to see him, and proceeded slowly and with long strides to pace the distance from the dolmen to the tree, noting down the measurements and compass bearings on a good-sized piece of paper. When the sergeant climbed over the last fence I looked at him with a startled expression, hurriedly pocketed the paper and walked forward to meet him.

"Rum-looking concern, that," he remarked, nodding at the dolmen and casting a suspicious glance round the field.

"Yes. Nothing to see, though," I replied indifferently, making as if to return to the road.

"May as well have a look at it," said Burbler; and he approached the venerable structure, and, having stared at it blankly for a while, remarked that it "looked as if it had been there some time".

"Getting on for three thousand years," said I.

"You don't say so!" he exclaimed. "Three thousand years! Gad! A repairing lease was worth something in those days."

He continued to cast puzzled glances at the dolmen and the old tree trunk, but failing to make anything of either of them, allowed himself ultimately to be led away.

On the following morning, having bolted my door, I prepared the final document, which consisted of a rough plan of the field, showing the dolmen and the tree and a number of dotted lines connecting them. At the bottom of the paper I wrote the following explanatory references:

"From dolmen to harp stone, 20 yards English cloth measure, due north.

From harp to first anchor 15…due west.

From first anchor to second anchor 5…due north.

…second anchor to third anchor $7\frac{1}{2}$…due east.

…third anchor to cross $7\frac{1}{2}$…due south.

Three and a half feet below the surface."

It is needless to say that this was all nonsense. But it had a fine, piratical, treasure-seeking appearance. I folded it neatly and laid it on a shelf in my cupboard with a couple of half-crowns on it; and having measured with my pocket dividers the exact distances from the half-crowns to the edges of the paper, I made a note of them and then went down to breakfast. Burbler had not yet left his room; but he appeared some ten minutes later with the most ludicrous expression of bewilderment that I have ever seen. I could have laughed in his face.

In the middle of breakfast I suddenly left the table and rushed upstairs as if I had forgotten something. Bolting my door, I carefully tested the position of the half-crowns on the sheet of paper; and when I found that it had changed by a full sixteenth of an inch, I knew that Burbler had gorged the bait, for Mrs Hodger had not left the kitchen. I accordingly pocketed the document and descended to finish my breakfast with renewed appetite. All the preliminaries were now arranged. I could reckon on getting rid of Burbler for an hour or so at least, and perhaps in the interval I might manage to lift or at any rate locate the treasure.

That very night I proceeded to carry my plan into execution. Soon after half past ten, the house being then all quiet, I stole silently (but not *too* silently, you understand) out of my room and descended to the cellar to provide myself with the needful appliances. A bundle of half-inch iron rods, each about four feet long and pointed at one end, stood in a corner; the remains, I suppose, of some kind of iron fence. One of these I selected as a sounding rod, and having annexed a good-sized hammer, a spade and a half-dozen clothes-pegs, I crept up from the cellar and listened for a few moments. The house was very silent, but once I thought I could distinguish faint sounds of stealthy movement above; on which I unbolted the front door and went out, shutting it behind me.

It was an ideal night for the purpose. The nearly full moon was covered by a thin veil of cloud, so that there was plenty of diffused light, and yet one was not too conspicuous; though, for that matter, there was not a soul about. The road was as deserted as the fields, and I arrived at the dolmen − by a slight detour, to avoid the neighbourhood of Farmer Babbage's bull − and without having seen a living creature.

Resting the spade against the dolmen, and taking a look through a large opening into the dark interior, I reflected awhile, studying my sketch plan and a pocket compass by the feeble light. There was no hurry. If Burbler was on my track, I must give him time to reach the spot. And yet I must not seem to dawdle if he had already arrived. I kept an eye on a clump of elders that would cover his approach, hoping to make out some signs of his presence; but the clouds now grew more dense and the light faded until the elders were no more than a vague dark mass. There was nothing for it but to begin and assume that Burbler was there.

I paced out the first line with long strides (and an eye on the elders) and at the end of it hammered one of the clothes-pegs into the ground. From this point I slowly paced to the "first anchor" and hammered in another peg; and so on until I had made the whole round and arrived at the spot marked on my sketch with the cross. And still there was no sign of Burbler.

A sudden, horrible suspicion entered my mind that I was going through all this tomfoolery without any audience at all. That was a frightful thought. But worse than that was the suspicion that now seized me and chilled my very blood, that Burbler might have taken advantage of my absence, and, even at this moment, while I was playing this fool's pantomime in an empty field, might be digging at the foot of the mulberry tree!

I broke out into a cold sweat. It was an awful dilemma. I couldn't stop my foolery for fear he might be watching after all; and yet I was in a fever to get back to the inn and see that nothing terrible was happening.

I had stuck the sounding rod in the ground and had the hammer poised for the first blow when a voice – a distinctly agricultural voice – broke the stillness of the night.

"Now then, you, what are you doing here at this time o' night?"

Naturally I thought that the unseen speaker was addressing me. But he wasn't. For a familiar voice answered sheepishly:

"Nothing in particular. Just having a walk round."

"Oh. Then you just take a walk out; out of my meadows. And you there! What are you up to?"

This question, bellowed in stentorian tones, was obviously addressed to me. It being impossible to ignore it, I walked towards the elders, whence the voice appeared to proceed, mumbling ambiguous explanations. By the fence under the trees I found Burbler and a stout, elderly man; presumably Farmer Babbage.

"Now then," said the latter, "you just come over the fence and I'll show you the way off my land. This here is the path."

"But," I protested "there is a bull in that meadow."

"Oh, he won't hurt you," said Babbage. "He's as quiet as a lamb, he is."

"Excuse me," said Burbler, "but I think I'd rather go some other way."

"You'll go along the footpath," the farmer began doggedly; but at this moment a roar like the blast of a colossal motor horn rent the silence, and a huge black shape emerged from the darkness of the meadow.

"He won't hurt you," repeated the farmer, getting over the fence with uncommon agility nevertheless. "He's as quiet as a – "

Now a bull is the most thick-headed of animals, literally and metaphorically. This particular behemoth had apparently selected Burbler as the object of assault, and he came on like — well, like a motor omnibus. I can't think of any more terrifying simile. But, of course, when he arrived Burbler wasn't there. But he didn't care for that. He proceeded to hurl a ton or so of beef and bones at the place where Burbler had been; and the consequence was that he hit the fence — a miserable row of rickety hurdles. And then the fence wasn't there.

What immediately followed I can't say, not being provided like the spider with eyes in my back. I only know that Farmer Babbage continued to asseverate "He won't hurt you", as distinctly as could be expected of a stout, elderly man who is crossing a field at about sixteen miles an hour. When I next looked back, from the shelter of another fence, Burbler appeared to be performing a kind of Druidical dance round the oak tree with the bull as an active and sympathetic acolyte.

Presently, taking advantage of a momentary lapse of attention on the part of the bull, the sergeant bolted across to the dolmen and shot in through the opening like a harlequin; and the last thing that I saw as I turned away was the bull with his nose thrust in through the opening of the dolmen uttering sonorous greetings to the sojourner within.

I made my way back to the inn with as little delay as possible. For the present Burbler was safe — safe, I mean, from my point of view. And when the bull released him he would probably lurk in the neighbourhood to see what I had been doing and to watch for my return. Still there was no time to be lost. I must find the treasure quickly or put off the search to another time.

I was still carrying the sounding rod and hammer, and that fact suggested to me the desirability of probing the ground under the mulberry tree before beginning to dig; for if Glynn's hoard lay deep down, out of reach of the four-foot rod, the amount of digging required would be greater than circumstances rendered possible on this occasion. Accordingly, having let myself in and bolted the door, I went straight through to the garden, and, taking my stand under the mulberry tree, looked up at the house. It was reasonable to suppose that the spot chosen would be as nearly as possible opposite the "maid from the sea on high", and, on this supposition, I stuck the point of the rod in the ground exactly in a line with the tablet, about a dozen feet from the tree, and drove it in with the hammer. It entered easily enough for the first eighteen inches. After that it became more and more difficult to drive in. But it met with no obstruction and after driving it in two feet six inches, I pulled it up and tried a fresh place in the same line.

I sounded in four or five places with the same discouraging result; and then I "struck soundings". It was at about two feet from the surface that I felt the resistance suddenly increase, and, when I had freed the rod a little, I could make out a definite solid obstacle. Eagerly I pulled up the rod, and, sticking the point in the ground about a foot nearer the tree, hammered it in. Again at about two feet down its progress was checked. There was certainly something there, and something of considerable size. Not a block of stone, as I could tell by working the rod up and down and striking the obstruction with the point, but apparently a massive wooden object, such as, for instance, a solidly-built chest.

I paused for a moment to consider. How long would it be before Burbler would be likely to return? That was a question to which I could give no answer. And meanwhile here was a solid something only a couple of feet down. With a pick and spade I could reach it in a few minutes. It might be a treasure chest or it might not, but in any case prudence whispered to me to take the opportunity lest I should never get another.

All a-tremble with excitement, I darted into the house and groped my way to the cellar. Quickly lighting a candle-lantern, I found my pick and a spade and having carried them up to the passage, I stood them against the wall and returned for the lantern. And then came the catastrophe. I was but halfway down the steps when someone leaped on me from behind, pinioning my arms and gripping my wrists. The impact was so violent that my assailant and I flew down the remaining steps and rolled together on the brick floor; and before I could extricate myself from the bear-like embrace, a chilly contact and a sharp, metallic snap told me that I was handcuffed and helpless.

"What the deuce is the meaning of this?" I exclaimed furiously.

"The meaning is," replied the too-familiar voice of Sergeant Burbler, "that you've been a bit too artful this time, Mr Cobb. Thought I was a regular greenhorn, didn't you? But I ain't. I've been watching you over the back gate for the last quarter of an hour. Now then, stop kicking, will you?"

I did stop, as a matter of fact; not voluntarily but in consequence of his lashing my ankles together. I heaped on him every objectionable epithet that a fairly retentive memory could recall; I called him a thief, a liar, a swindler and a traitor. But he was perfectly impassive. With a calm air of business he passed a cord round my arms at the elbows, and, having tied it behind, dragged me to an oaken chest, on which he seated me with my face towards the door.

"Now, Mr Cobb," said he, "if you'll excuse me, I'll just run away and attend to that little business outside. I'll leave you the lantern, as I have one of my own."

With this he departed, bolting the door after him; and very soon there came in, through the little grated ventilators, the sound of a pick – my pick! –plied with furious energy.

I could have wept with rage and disappointment. Here was a pretty end to all my scheming! I had played the jackal that this mangy Scotland Yard lion might gobble up the prey!

After a time I grew calmer. The sound of the pick continued from without and I listened to it with growing resignation. Presently it intermitted and then I heard the sharper sound of the hammer striking the sounding rod. Not a soothing sound it might be thought; and yet it comforted me. For it told me that what I had struck was certainly not the treasure and that, so far, the villain Burbler had drawn a blank. Supposing the treasure was not there, after all! What an anticlimax that would be! And what an awful fool the Sergeant would look!

The old proverb that "the wish is father to the thought" now received an apt illustration in the psychic phenomena that my reflections exhibited. So long as the hidden treasure was potentially mine, I had dwelt rather exclusively on the evidence that it was there; but now that it was potentially Burbler's I found myself dwelling rather on the facts that suggested that it was not there. And, really, when one came to consider the facts, it did look as if I had jumped at a somewhat hasty conclusion. The harp and the cross and the anchors three, which I had brushed aside as not so very material, now began to loom up as factors of prime importance. It seemed as if the circumstances required careful reconsideration.

And now, for the first time, I began to give that mystical jingle of old Simon's really systematic thought. I went over it line by line and applied its quaint phrases to the present conditions. And the more I did so, the less they seemed to fit. Gradually, I came to the conclusion that I had made a false shot; a mere hasty guess. That the foot of the mulberry tree could not be the place where the treasure was buried at all, and that the whole of the data needed to be revised.

And all the time, the sound of the pick and spade drifted in monotonously through the little grating.

A couple of hours passed. Slowly my ideas, from a formless ambiguity, began to crystallize into something like definite shape. A few minutes more of concentrated thought and I should have evolved a more or less complete solution of the riddle. But at that moment the sound of the pick ceased; heavy footsteps clumped along the passage; the cellar door was unbolted and flung open; and Sergeant Burbler entered, wiping his forehead with a very dirty hand.

"Look here, Mr Cobb" he said, irritably, "do you know where that stuff is, or don't you?"

"No, I'm hanged if I do," said I, "unless you've got it."

"Well, I haven't. And I don't believe it was ever there."

"Neither do I. But you haven't wasted your time, you know, Sergeant. It might have been there. It was just as well to make sure. I'm very much obliged to you for all the trouble you've taken. Perhaps

you wouldn't mind unfastening these things now; then I can help you
to fill up the hole."

Sulkily and with an air of deep depression, Burbler released me
from the handcuffs and the lashings. He offered no apology for his
conduct, and I asked for none. When I had stretched myself and
secured another spade, we went out into the garden to repair damages.
Under the mulberry tree yawned a wide and deep pit, bridged by the
thick root on which my sounding rod had struck. The sergeant and I
fell to at once with our spades to fill up the hole; and though we both
worked with a will, it was with very different feelings. Burbler was
silent and gloomy. Perhaps he was considering what he should say to
Mrs Hodger. As to me, the "might have been" was with me no more,
but only that which yet might be.

As I gleefully shovelled in the earth it seemed that perhaps success
might, after all, rise, Phœnix-like, from the ashes of a dead and gone
failure.

CHAPTER SIX

The Magic Mirror

Human knowledge may be roughly divided into two categories: that which we acquire at school, and that which is of some practical use. Occasionally the two divisions overlap, as in the case of schoolmasters or crammers, who contrive to squeeze a livelihood out of their schooling; but in general they are completely separate. No academic course would have helped me one jot to solve the riddle of Simon Glynn's treasure, whereas one or two items of somewhat out-of-the-way knowledge – but I am rather anticipating. Let me tell the story in its proper sequence.

It was the morning after the excavation under the mulberry tree. That had failed. Previous attempts of mine had failed; and the explorations of innumerable treasure-seekers before me had failed. And all for the same simple reason. None of us had given the problem sufficient preliminary thought. We had all, apparently, jumped from one or two clues to the solution; and the solution had turned out to be the wrong one every time.

I walked up and down the little green in front of the Royal George, and my fellow lodger sat in the orchard at the side of the house in his shirtsleeves and a pair of hideous carpet slippers, reading yesterday's paper and keeping an eye on me. For Burbler was no longer an investigator; his rôle was to shadow me and suck my brains. Even now, he was watching me like a cat, to see if I looked as if I had hit on another clue.

I paced to and fro, thinking profoundly. There should be no more guesswork. I would go over the whole set of facts from the beginning and consider them systematically to see if I could not evolve some theory that would fit them all.

As I paced to and fro, deep in thought, I passed and repassed the signpost. And thus, glancing at it at each turn, I noticed for the first time what a very singular post it was. And then I began to look at it more particularly and note those peculiarities in which it differed from other signposts that I had seen.

In the first place, it was not planted in the ground, but set in a socket in a great block of stone. Then its lower third was encased in lead sheathing, very neatly finished, though now disguised by paint. The top was protected by a long iron cap to which the ironwork of the sign was attached, and the wooden shaft itself showed, through the crust of paint, obscure traces of strap-work carving. Looking attentively at the iron scrollwork, I made out with some difficulty – for here, too, generations of painters had left their marks – four small figures, which together made the date 1636. Then the ironwork was actually that originally put up by Glynn; and it looked as if the post itself was the original one, which, indeed, it might easily have been, for, with its stone base, its lead sheathing, and its iron cap, it was so perfectly protected from damp that it might still last for a century or two.

But why this extraordinary care to preserve the wooden post? Oak was not such a very costly commodity in Glynn's time, and the stone base must have cost more than a dozen posts. Why, then, these elaborate precautions?

I turned this question over as I walked up and down with my eyes fixed meditatively on the sign. And then, in a flash, I saw it: and called myself a whole battalion of idiots for not having seen it before.

I looked up, I say, at the sign, which showed a portrait of a royal personage who wore a tie-wig and had a face somewhat like a well-scrubbed mangold-wurzel – George the third, in fact. But it was obvious that in Glynn's day the sign of this tavern could not have been the Royal George. And if one asked what the original sign was, the answer came at once from the sculptured mermaid on the back gable. That elaborate panel was not a cottage tablet but a tavern sign. Hence, too, the reason why that panel was at the back of the house; for the front had the painted mermaid on the signboard. And, of course, it was this sign and not the sculptured figure that was the "Maid from the Sea on high".

But, if this was so, where was the "tree" that was referred to in the rhyme? Again the answer was obvious. In Glynn's day the old use of the word "tree" as a synonym for "wood" still lingered; as, indeed, it does today in such words as roof-tree, chess-tree, trestle-tree, axle-tree, treenail (a wooden peg), and many others. Moreover, in those days, a large post actually was a tree; an entire trunk of suitable size shaped with the adze. The signpost itself was the tree.

And now I understood – or believed I understood – those elaborate arrangements to preserve the post from decay, and to avoid disturbance of the ground if it did decay. The treasure was hidden at the foot of the post; and those precautions were taken to guard against its chance discovery by workmen engaged in carrying out repairs. For Simon had specially stipulated for "wit" on the part of the finder.

So far, it all looked very complete and consistent. But this was not to be guesswork. I must fairly consider the objections. And there were two serious defects in this theory. In the first place there was no vestige of any harp or cross; and in the second the "ankores three" were conspicuously absent. These seemed to be fatal objections to my theory as to the whereabouts of the treasure, and, for the moment, I was a good deal discouraged. But then I remembered that this was a riddle intentionally made difficult, and that if its solution had been more obvious it would not have remained, after all these years, for me to solve. Accordingly I addressed myself to the first difficulty; that of the harp and cross.

Now, the association of ideas presents some very curious phenomena. You may have two or more separate ideas, each of which, by itself, is meaningless and vague; but bring them together and forthwith they yield a compound idea of the utmost significance. So it happened now. The words "harp and cross" had, from the first, vaguely suggested to me some half-forgotten incident which I could not recall. And again, when I had read on Simon Glynn's monument the motto, "God with us", I had felt some chord of memory vibrate, but had been too preoccupied to analyze the impression. Just now, however, I was in an analytical mood and I recalled both these vague recollections and asked myself what they meant. And then, in a moment, the two ideas ran together and led me back straight to their joint origin.

The incident occurred in front of one of the cabinets of a coin-collecting friend. He had just taken out a Commonwealth twenty-shilling piece and handed it to me.

"There, Cobb," he had said, "that is a piece of old Oliver's. Observe the pious inscription, 'God with us'. This is the coin, you know, that Pepys refers to as 'the old Harp and Cross money'. "

I recalled it now, perfectly, and the appearance of the piece, with the device of the Harp and Cross and the motto, "God with us". This, of course, was the money that was struck when Simon Glynn was at the mint.

It was all clear enough now. The Harp and Cross were not marks on the hiding place of the treasure. They were on the treasure itself. The words in the rhyme, were, in fact, a trap set by the "whimsicall" Simon to catch the unwary; and the unwary had been caught in very considerable numbers.

The difficulty of the "ankores three" now seemed to melt away of itself; for the quibble of the Harp and Cross suggested a simple solution. It was a pun on Simon's coat of arms, the three anchors; as was, indeed, suggested by the ambiguous spelling of the word "ankores", which left the reader free to render it "anchors" or "ankers" according to his judgment. For my part, I had no doubt whatever. Here was old Simon's tavern in the midst of the smuggling country with a tidal river flowing past its very door. Many an anker of Dutch liquor must have drifted up from Sandwich in those good old days, and many an empty anker must have cumbered the cellar. What more natural than that the jovial Simon should have used these convenient vessels for treasure chests?

I trust that I am not a conceited man; but I must admit that I paid myself a few handsome compliments on my ingenuity. For here I had a complete and reasonable solution of that cryptic rhyme which had puzzled generations of eager treasure-seekers. Three ankers filled with gold Harp and Cross money buried at the foot of the signpost on top of which swung the sign of the mermaid. That was the solution. It was simple, and it covered every word of the rhyme, which no previous solution had done. All that remained was to gather the reward of my ingenuity. Others had "stepped over"; it was for me, the chosen one, to "take itt" and fulfil Simon's prophecy as to his legatee.

This was all very well. But "itt" was by no means conveniently situated. The signpost stood some twenty yards from the house at the side of a public road, and was, moreover, planted in a block of stone weighing a ton or two. To disinter the ankers would involve mining operations on a scale that would attract the attention, not only of Burbler and Mrs Hodger, but of the whole countryside.

Here was another setback. But I was not daunted by it; a moment's reflection convinced me that the difficulty – which was as great in Glynn's time as now – must have been provided for. Simon could never have meant the successful candidate to dig up the signpost. There must be some easier means of access to the treasure – probably from the inside of the house. I had seen, at Elham Manor, what Glynn could do in the way of secret chambers and hidden doors; there was nothing for it but to explore the interior of the inn. But it was a little disappointing, just when I thought I had solved the riddle, to have a new and difficult problem presented, especially since I knew that every movement of mine would be eagerly watched by Burbler.

And then it was that, puzzling over this new difficulty, I had a really brilliant idea; an inspiration, in fact.

It had often struck me as a little odd that Glynn should have elected to engrave his doggerel on the frame of a mirror. It was very inconvenient, for the inscription had to be zigzagged round the four sides in an awkwardly narrow space. A salver, or even a tankard or goblet, would have offered a much more convenient surface and would not have broken up the verse. Why had he chosen a mirror frame? Had he any special reason for his choice? And if he must have had a mirror, why a silver one? Glass mirrors were in common use in his time.

The study of optics has always had somewhat of a fascination for me; and especially that branch of it which deals with the quaint and the marvellous; in fact, with what one may call "optical magic". And thus it happened that as I cogitated on Simon Glynn's mirror with its cryptic rhyme, a very curious suggestion occurred to me.

I wonder how many people are acquainted with that queer product of old Japan, the "magic mirror"? A good many specimens exist. I have had the privilege of examining one or two myself. In its usual form, it is a smallish hand mirror with a face of polished speculum metal and a richly-ornamented back; and the centre of the back is always occupied by a device – usually the figure of a dragon or bird – deeply and elaborately chased. Used in the ordinary way, it presents nothing unusual. If you look into one, you see a reflection of your face – just an ordinary reflection, quite plain and free from distortion. But if you catch a gleam of sunlight on the polished face and throw the reflection on a smooth surface such as a whitewashed wall, a most remarkable and uncanny effect is produced. The device on the back of the mirror is plainly visible in the patch of reflected light on the wall, where it appears as a dark shape with a bright halo. It sounds like a sheer impossibility, and to an observer who isn't "in the know" it looks like black magic. The sort of magic, by the way, that Simon Glynn would have enjoyed. Which brings me back to my brilliant idea: Supposing Glynn's mirror should be a magic mirror!

These meditations had brought me unconsciously to a halt at the end of the green, opposite the orchard. Happening to glance up, I became aware of Burbler, sitting erect in his chair and eyeing me intently. I suppose that something of the excitement that surged within me was apparent in my face. That, in short, my expression had suggested a fresh clue.

Hang Burbler! This spying and watching was distracting to a degree. And it was worse than distracting. I was now in a fever to test my new idea; but I wasn't going to test it in Burbler's presence. There was only one thing to be done. I had my hat and boots on and a sovereign or so in my pockets. I had better take a flying start while I had the chance.

I took one or two more turns up and down the green to put Burbler off his guard; then, when I reached the end of my walk, instead of turning yet again, I quickened my pace and strode off along the road. As I passed the orchard Burbler leaped from his chair, dropped his newspaper and made a bolt for the house – obviously to put on his boots and coat; and I, having walked quickly to a bend in the road, vaulted over a stile and ran at the top of my speed along the footpath that formed the short cut into Canterbury.

As I ran, I continued my speculations on Simon Glynn's mirror; and the more I thought about it the more likely did it seem that the little silver plate held the final clue. For, after all, the miracle of the Japanese mirror is quite a simple affair and I expect many of the old working goldsmiths and silversmiths knew all about it. It is just a matter of the hardening of metal under a hammered tool.

If you work a device, with chasing tool and hammer, on the back of a plate of annealed metal, that device will show through quite distinctly on the face in slight relief. If this relief is ground away on a wet stone, the device will, of course, disappear. But it has not really gone. For though the face of the plate is now perfectly even, the device is still there in the substance of the metal. Wherever the tool has struck, the metal is hardened right through; and as soon as the face is polished, the hardness of the worked area will cause the device to reappear. Its projection will be so infinitesimal as to be imperceptible to the eye, but it will be quite sufficient to deflect rays of parallel light and cause the device to be visible in the reflection. Even if the design is stoned off the back as well as the face, the hardness will remain and the device will still show in the reflection though it has disappeared from both surfaces of the plate. So that the process would offer a plan after the very heart of a whimsically secretive man like Simon Glynn.

By the time I entered the streets of Canterbury, I had shaped an immediate course of action. My first objective was a shop in which I had seen some very efficient-looking electric torches; and, as I knew the price and had the money ready in my hand, the purchase was only a matter of seconds. With the torch in my pocket, I made a beeline for the museum, and, passing through the galleries as rapidly as I dared, proceeded to the room in the annexe in which Glynn's mirror was exhibited.

It was a critical moment. An inopportune visitor or attendant would have spoiled all; for Burbler would, no doubt, come straight to the museum, as the only place of which he knew as connected with our common quest. But fortune was kind. The room and the adjoining corridor were empty, and the mirror stood in its position on a side table. I took the precaution to open and inspect the curtained sedan chair, which was the only possible hiding place in the room; and, having shut it again, I looked round, listened, and then, with a thumping heart, approached the mirror.

The little silver object stood, as I have said, on a high side table, inclined at an angle of forty-five degrees – just the right position for me. I gave its face a hasty wipe with my silk handkerchief, stepped back a couple of paces, pointed the bull's-eye of my torch and pressed the switch. As the beam of light fell on the mirror, a bright oblong patch appeared on the ceiling above it. But not a mere, plain patch of reflected light. On the bright space I could make out in dim and shadowy, but quite legible, lettering, the words:

"Pull out ye 3rd Stepp."

I switched off the light, slipped the torch into my pocket and made my way out of the room as quickly as I had entered. For now I knew all that I wanted to know, and my business was to escape Burbler, at any rate until I had decided on my next move. And I was none too soon. As I passed a staircase window, I saw the sergeant taking the entrance steps two at a time, and I had barely slipped into the picture gallery when he flew past the door on his way to the "mirror room".

As his steps died away I came forth from the gallery and hurried out of the building before he should return in search of me. My immediate need was that of a quiet place where I could reflect on what I had just learned and decide what to do next. The streets were not very restful with Burbler prowling up and down in search of me;

eventually I drifted into the cathedral precincts, and sought sanctuary in a remote corner of the cloisters.

"Pull out ye 3rd Stepp!"

I smiled as I repeated to myself that quaint message, whispered to me, as it were, in confidence across the gulf of two centuries. How like the pleasant and "whimsicall" Simon! For, of course, that direction, intelligible enough to me, would have been perfectly meaningless to anyone else. The question would have arisen, "what third step?" But I understood. The direction was addressed to the person of "wit" who had read the riddle. To me, in fact. And I knew that there was only one set of steps that bore any relation to the foot of the signpost; but those steps I knew very well indeed, having sat opposite them, manacled and bound, for a matter of three hours. The cellar steps of the Royal George (late The Mermaid) inn answered the conditions exactly; and since there were five of them, the middle step was the third whichever way one counted.

It was all plain sailing so far. I should pull out the third step and probably find the entrance to a forgotten smugglers' hiding hole under the signpost. That was what it looked like. But there was Burbler. He was the fly in the ointment; and a mighty big fly, too; a regular bluebottle. If he spotted me going down to the cellar, he would be on my heels in a moment, and then the whole thing would be blown upon. I should be lucky if I got even a share of the treasure, for Burbler had shown himself a greedy, unscrupulous rascal.

No. Before I ventured to approach the hiding place I must, by hook or by crook, get rid of Burbler. That was the pressing necessity of the moment.

I have remarked on a previous occasion that necessity is the mother of invention. The aphorism is not mine. It has been said before; and I merely quote it as an appropriate observation. Because, at the end of an hour's pacing of the cloisters and after enough concentrated thought to furnish out a royal commission, I had evolved quite a pretty little scheme.

There is more than one kind of magic mirror. I have described the less known variety. A more familiar kind, known to us in our childhood and sold in the toy shops of that prehistoric age, had somewhat different properties. You presented it to your most intimate and valued friend and invited him to breathe on it in order that he might see himself as others saw him. He accordingly breathed on it; whereupon there appeared on its surface a lifelike representation of a donkey's head.

There was nothing miraculous about it. I learned the secret of manufacture from a Hebrew gentleman who sold second-hand furniture. He was in the habit of writing the prices on his looking-glasses with a piece of soap, and he made the interesting discovery that if he wiped off the soap-marked figures with a dry cloth and polished the glass, although the latter then appeared perfectly clear and bright, yet the figures would reappear quite distinctly if the glass was breathed upon.

Now here was a valuable piece of knowledge – not acquired through academic channels. It seemed to me that, with its aid, I might treat Sergeant Burbler to a little communication from the late Simon Glynn. And if the communication were discreetly worded, it might furnish him with enough occupation to keep him out of mischief while I transacted my business with the cellar steps. There was only one really serious difficulty. Burbler had got to be made to read that mystic message from the long-departed Simon; and I didn't quite see how to do it.

From the cathedral precincts I stole out warily into Burgate Street and wandered about until I encountered an oil shop, where I purchased a small tablet of soap. Cutting a slice from this, I shaped it to the form of a moderately sharp crayon which I carefully wrapped in paper and dropped in my pocket. Then I executed a highly strategic advance on the museum. It was a delicate affair, for if I ran against Burbler it was quite probable that he would freeze on, and then I should have to postpone my little manœuvre; which would be most exasperating. For I need hardly say that I was suffering an agony of impatience to get back to the inn and see what was behind the "third Stepp".

I walked up to the entrance, and, after a precautionary look round, bolted in. There was no sign of Burbler. Breathlessly I threaded my way through the galleries, ready at a moment's notice to slip behind a door or showcase, until I came to the corridor that led into the "mirror room". Here I paused for a moment, looking through into the room. A party of American tourists was in occupation at the moment, but otherwise the room seemed to be empty. I accordingly entered boldly, and, while the Americans were taking their lightning impressions of the exhibits, I passed the time by examining the interior of the sedan chair – to make sure that the place really was empty, after all.

The Americans, having filled their intellectual crops with characteristic rapidity, departed, leaving me in sole possession: whereupon I took another glance round, shut the door of the sedan chair, and stepped over to the mirror. There was no time to be lost. Burbler might arrive at any moment and rob me of my opportunity. Taking out my soap crayon, I wrote carefully on the silver surface in antique, but very legible characters the following mystical words:

"Under ye floare of ye litell blew Chamber."

I was not very satisfied with the result, for, owing to the dryness of the soap, the writing was almost invisible. However, when I had polished it off with my handkerchief until every sign of it was gone and then breathed heavily on the mirror, I was quite reassured; for the inscription stood out with the distinctness of engraving. But only for one instant. As the steamy film faded away, the writing faded with it; and, when I turned away, the surface of the mirror was as bright and blank as before the guileful crayon touched it.

The problem now was how to catch Burbler – or, rather, how to let him catch me. It would take some nice management, and I mustn't be caught prematurely. I had a roughly-shaped plan, and, as that plan was connected with the public library – which was in the same building – I made my way thither to think it over. I looked round a little anxiously as I entered the reference room and was half-relieved and half-disappointed to find that the sergeant was not there. I didn't want him until I had completed my little preparations, but, on the other hand, it would be an absolute disaster if he had given up the pursuit and gone back to the inn.

But again fortune favoured me. Before reconnoitring the shelves, I happened to glance out of the window at the street below. And there he was, ostensibly gaping into a shop window, but actually keeping a watch on the entrance of the museum. So I shouldn't have to go out and angle for him in the town if I could attract his attention.

I snatched a large volume from a shelf and, going close to the window, pored over the open book with as intent an expression as I could assume, watching Burbler out of the tail of my eye. For some time he failed to notice me, but continued, to my annoyance, to glance furtively up and down the street and across at the museum entrance. But at last he caught sight of me; on which his interest in the shop window lapsed and he darted across the road.

I replaced the book on the shelf, and, running my eye along the volumes of the Encyclopædia Britannica, selected the one marked "Mem – Mos", and laid it on the table. Seating myself, I produced a sheet of paper and a pencil, and, opening the volume at the article "Mirror", assumed an air of eager preoccupation. Presently the door opened softly. I didn't dare to look round, but my ear gave me the information that I wanted. For Burbler's favourite boots had a peculiar soft creak, almost entirely confined to the right boot; and when I heard that creak proceeding stealthily round the room behind me I knew that the critical moment had come. If he spoke to me my plan would have failed and I should have to devise some other.

I had written large and legibly at the head of my paper the words "Experiments on metallic mirrors", and I now began to copy out chance sentences from the article in a much smaller handwriting. Meanwhile the creaky boot lingered behind me opposite the book-shelves and presently began to approach by easy stages until I was conscious of someone standing close behind my chair. I scribbled frantically, almost perspiring with anxiety. Would he take the bait? He was certainly looking over my shoulder; he could hardly fail to make out the heading to my notes. But would he adopt the suggestion that I was offering? It was a very obvious one and he was no fool; but there was the danger that he might fail to reason as I was trying to make him reason. And then he wouldn't do what I wanted him to do.

The creak softly retreated. I heard a book returned to the shelf behind me; and then that tell-tale boot moved stealthily but rather quickly towards the entrance. A door opened and closed; and, listening intently, I could distinguish the creak moving away pretty quickly in the direction of the galleries. It really looked as if the worthy sergeant had swallowed the bait.

I didn't act precipitately. I gave him a good five minutes' start in case he should be hampered by the presence of visitors. Then I replaced the volume, and, pocketing my notes, set forth on my third visit to the shrine of Simon Glynn. I have never been more anxious or less confident. For it was a pure gamble. I had endeavoured to convey into Burbler's mind the impression that I was about to make some experiments on Glynn's mirror; and I now had to act on the assumption that I had conveyed that impression and that Burbler would take some measures to be present at the experiments. Whereas I might have failed utterly. And to make things more disquieting, I had discovered, too late, that the article in the Encyclopædia actually contained a brief description of Chinese and Japanese magic mirrors. However, it couldn't be helped.

The "mirror room" was fortunately in its normal state of emptiness. I stole in with a secret and nervous air and looked round. I hardly dared to look at the sedan chair, but yet I couldn't resist just one instantaneous glance as I entered. And that glance yielded distinct encouragement. For the door of the chair was not completely shut. But when I had looked in last I had been careful to shut it; and that door had a snap catch which could not be opened from within. Two very significant facts. *Verbum sap.*

I stole up to the mirror, and, opening my mouth wide, breathed noisily two or three times. The polished surface clouded and the soaped inscription leaped out and grinned in my face. There was no possibility of missing it. I stared at it fatuously for a second or two; then I turned and walked quickly on tiptoe out of the room and down the corridor. But instead of turning away down the next gallery,

I quietly slipped behind a large harem screen of Cairene lattice-work which stood at the end of the corridor. Through the chinks of the lattice I could command a view of part of the room, including the sedan chair and the mirror, though quite invisible myself; and I accordingly glued my eye to one of the chinks and watched in an agony of suspense.

Several seconds passed. And every second I grew more and yet more nervous. And then came the blessed relief. Very slowly and softly the door of the sedan chair opened and out popped a head – Burbler's, of course. He looked round and listened for a moment, and, seeing no one in the room or corridor, forth he came like a cautious hermit crab emerging from a whelk shell. Shutting the door silently he stole across to the mirror and bent over it.

I stared through the lattice in positive ecstasy. There was no doubt what he was doing; his muzzle was within four inches of the mirror and his mouth gaped like that of a moribund haddock. But he didn't stay long in that position. One moment I saw him gaping at the mirror; the next he was coming down the corridor like Farmer Babbage's bull.

I gave him a few seconds' start. I heard him stamp through two galleries and down a flight of stairs and then I took up the pursuit. When I came out into the street, he was just turning the corner, evidently making for the short cut back to the inn. Taking a different turning, I ran as hard as I could until I reached the outskirts of the town, when I slowed down into a jaunty walk. Presently Burbler came in sight, stepping out as if he was in for the one-mile handicap – as, in fact, he was – on a path which joined mine a couple of hundred yards farther on. As soon as he saw me, he broke into a furious run, and, of course, I followed suit. But I let him draw ahead so that he reached the junction first; by which I secured the advantage of keeping him in sight and seeing him knock his shins on the stile. I could even hear his comments on the circumstance – which seemed to reflect unfairly on the constructor of the stile – and note a singular alteration in his gait; but I let him maintain the lead and even increase it, for there was no sense in fatiguing myself unnecessarily.

We both entered the inn by the back door in quick succession and we both made straight for the little blue room – Burbler's bedroom. When I arrived, the door was securely bolted on the inside and earth-quaky sounds proceeded from within. It was a mercy that our landlady, Mrs Hodger, was stone-deaf and kept no assistants!

"Go away!" roared Burbler as I fumbled at the handle. "Go away! I'm busy."

I sniggered softly. Busy he evidently was! But he would be more busy before he'd finished. For it was a small room and it contained a medium-sized bed, three large chests of drawers, a washstand and a massive standing cupboard, besides other trifles. What there wasn't in that room was space to swing a cat. Not, of course, that Burbler wanted to swing a cat. He only wanted to take up the floor. But a floor of massive oak plank is a bit of a handful in itself without the contents of a pantechnicon on top of it. Burbler wasn't going to be one of the unemployed. Busy indeed!

I thumped gleefully on the door, and, under cover of the noise and Burbler's profanities from within, quietly shot the two strong bolts on the outside. Then I gave Burbler a few words in season through the keyhole, and, having listened unmoved to his obscene responses, I took myself off to attend to my own little business.

And now that the excitement of the chase – so to speak – was over, a sudden chill of fear came over me. Supposing that I had misread the riddle after all! What a frightful anticlimax that would be, after bottling up my rival so neatly, too. I ran down to the cellar almost sick with apprehension and only just had presence of mind enough to bolt myself in.

There was no doubt as to which end of the third step I must pull, for one end was embedded in the wall, while the other offered a very handy corner to lay hold of. This corner I grasped and gave one or two vigorous pulls; but the massive hardwood slab, which appeared to be fixed in its place with large treenails, gave no sign of yielding. Then I fetched a heavy mallet from the cupboard where the tools were kept, and, laying my folded handkerchief on the corner of the step, delivered two or three sharp taps. At the first tap it became evident that the treenails were dummies, for the step began to separate from its frame. A few more taps brought it fairly away so that I was able to swing it round and then lift it out bodily, leaving a large oblong hole with a dark cavity beyond.

Lighting the candle-lantern, I held it inside the hole. The cavity was walled and floored with brick and seemed to extend away to the left; and as the air, though close and earthy, did not seem to be foul, I climbed through the opening and began cautiously to creep along a narrow passage. It was quite a long passage. I had proceeded fully fifteen yards – in the direction of the signpost, as I suddenly realized – when I came to a short flight of brick steps, beyond which the passage opened on either side into a range of vaults, each of which was occupied by rows of casks or by racks of strange-looking, squat, short-necked bottles.

There was something rather uncanny in the aspect of these casks and bottles, full, as I suspected, of contraband liquor and now mantled with the soft, grey dust of centuries. But I had little attention to bestow on them, for now the light of the lantern fell on a much more interesting object. Near the end of the passage was a large stone baluster like the pillar of a sundial; on top of it was a square slab of stone; and on the slab, three small kegs. They were not really ankers. The opportunity for a pun had tempted old Simon to stretch the facts, but that was a small matter. I ran forward eagerly to examine the booty.

The kegs were of rather unusual finish and strength and were fitted with thick copper hoops. All three were broached, for the heads and the spare hoops lay by their sides; and each keg was covered by a tile, thickly coated with dust. I had those tiles off in a twinkling, and found, as I had expected, a layer of neatly arranged gold coins, each set so as to exhibit the Harp and Cross device and the motto, "God with us".

I drew a deep breath of relief. The lurking fear that some previous explorer had visited the hiding place was now set at rest. And yet I was conscious of a slight disappointment – such is the avarice begotten of treasure-hunting. For, after all, the promised ankers had dwindled to little kegs of barely a gallon capacity. It could only be a matter of a thousand or two at the most. And yet, perhaps, it was as well; for I could probably carry these, one at a time, to the boat (which was the means of transport that I had selected); whereas I could not even have moved an anker filled with gold coins. Here I lifted one of the kegs, to test its weight; and a most horrible shock I received. For though it was inconveniently heavy for hasty removal, it was not heavy enough for a keg of gold. I grabbed up a handful of the gold coins; and behold! my fist was half full of sawdust!

Horror! Was this another of Simon's beastly jokes?

I thrust my hand deep into the keg. No coins could I feel with my groping fingers, but plenty of sawdust; and embedded in it a number of rough, irregularly-shaped objects, one of which I fished out and held to the lantern. And then my chagrin was changed into delirious joy. For the object was a massive thumb-ring set with a great green stone; apparently an emerald, and worth a hatful of gold. I dived into another keg and brought up a pendant set with large, rose-cut diamonds; and the third yielded at the first cast a beautiful miniature of an elderly man – perhaps Simon himself – with a broad, diamond-studded frame.

I waited to investigate no more. Quickly heading up the kegs, I slipped on the hoops and tapped them into place with one of the tiles. The little casks were all prepared for convenient removal, for the end hoops were fitted with strong copper rings through which were rove stout slings of rawhide; and these, thanks to the protection from rats and vermin offered by the stone pillar, were perfectly sound and strong. I lifted the kegs down, and, finding that I could just stagger under the weight of the three, was about to make my way out, when, suddenly, I bethought me of Burbler. I should have to carry my booty out to the landing stage, for there was no time to move the boat to a safer place; and it was just possible that Burbler might see me from the window; and if he did, he would certainly give chase. I should have to land somewhere, and as he could easily keep up with the boat and observe where I landed, I should have no chance of getting away, encumbered with so heavy a burden.

What was to be done?

I thought furiously for a few moments, and then I saw the solution. I must have yet another red herring to draw across my trail if necessary. The suggestion of the plan came from a pile of empty kegs – the memorials of many a forgotten smuggling trip. The wine bins were full of sawdust and a number of short lengths of rusty chain were stacked in a corner. I don't know what they had been used for, but I know that they came in mighty useful just now; for it took me but a few minutes to fill up three of the empty kegs with them and to add a packing of sawdust and head them up. Then I was ready to start.

I carried the six kegs out into the cellar, and uncommonly heavy they were, especially those filled with chain. Then I carefully replaced the step and banged it home until there was no sign of its having been disturbed; after which, having put away the mallet, I proceeded to the actual embarkation. Caution suggested that I should take up the three dummy kegs first, as I should have to leave them unguarded in the boat while I fetched the others, and I accordingly carried them up. It was growing dusk by this time, and a cloudy evening too, but not dark enough to cover my movements from Burbler if he should chance to look out of the window. But he didn't. I got the three dummies stowed in the boat safely and returned unobserved; and loud rumblifications from the Blue Room told me that my rival was still busy.

I had just brought up the second three, after blowing out the candle in the lantern, and was close to the landing stage, when a cessation of the noises from above caused me to look up. And it was lucky that I did; for there was Burbler at the window in his shirt-sleeves, gazing at me with an expression that would have curdled a can of sterilized milk. Stock-still he stood for a couple of seconds and then vanished; and as I bolted to the landing stage, I heard him furiously shaking the door in his efforts to get out.

I lowered the kegs into the boat, jumped in myself, cast off the painter, snatched up the sculls and pulled away frantically downstream against the weakening flood tide. And as I moved away into the dusk, the shattering of glass and the raising of a window told me that

Burbler had given up the door in favour of the easy drop down into the garden.

The gathering gloom and the mists that were rising in the water-meadows made it difficult to see if I was being pursued; but I had no doubt that Burbler was following the boat under cover of the scattered bushes and the embankments of the dykes. I turned the situation over as I plied the sculls. The only practicable place at which to land was Grove Ferry, some miles farther down; and Burbler knew that and would be there when I arrived. He would know that I couldn't carry that weight across country.

But there was one place where I should lose him for a minute or two; a place where the river made a horseshoe bend, enclosing a little peninsula that was cut off from the mainland by a broad and deep dyke. The dyke was impassable as I knew from experience, and the fringing willows would screen me for a few minutes. At that place, then, the next act must be played.

It took me over half an hour to get there, during which I twice caught a glimpse of a shadowy figure climbing over a dyke gate and instantly vanishing – presumably behind a bank. At length I passed the entrance to the broad dyke. The river swept away to the right and a forest of willows rose to cut me off from any possible observation. Instantly I ran the boat on the opposite bank – with the river between me and Burbler – and, making fast to an overhanging tree, landed the three genuine kegs and carried them into a meadow. Staggering along the bank of a straight dyke (or drainage ditch), I bore my burden to the first gate; and here I regretfully sank them to the muddy bottom in about two feet of water. Returning to the river and carefully noting the position of the tree to which I had made fast the boat, I cast off the painter and once more took to the sculls, pulling with all my might to make up for lost time; and as I passed the outlet of the broad dyke, I had the satisfaction of making out quite distinctly a human head in a hat which I recognized, peering over the low embankment.

It was fully half a mile lower down that I made my second landing. At that point was a ruinous hovel – once, no doubt, a shepherd's hut, but now disused. Here, I thought I would secrete the three dummies and then pull back and recover my treasure, by which time Burbler would have purloined the dummies and made off, leaving the coast clear for me to pull down to Grove Ferry.

It was a neat scheme. But it didn't come off quite as I had expected; for I made the mistake of going ashore to reconnoitre; and I had hardly reached the hut when I heard a loud splash, and when I looked round, there was that confounded Burbler in the boat pulling away upstream like clockwork. It was frightfully annoying; for now it was I who was on the wrong side of the river. Moreover Burbler would discover the fraud prematurely and then I should have him shadowing me again and preventing me from recovering my treasure.

But this would never do. Those kegs might be discovered at daybreak by some shepherd or herdsman. Somehow I must recover them tonight and hide them more securely; and with this resolution, I faced about and headed upstream with the intention of making for Fordwich Bridge.

I set off at a leisurely pace, keeping by the river until I was cut off from it by the big dyke, which I followed to the spot where it joined the river. And here I got a great surprise; for as I came out on the riverside path, I perceived a man a little distance ahead hurrying in the same direction. Now as no one had passed me, this man must have come from the river. With a sudden suspicion, I broke into a run and overtook him. And my suspicion was correct. It was Burbler. He thought I should return to the inn, and he meant to be there when I arrived.

"Hallo, Mr Cobb!" he exclaimed. "You taking an evening walk, too!"

"Now, look here, Burbler," said I. "What have you done with those kegs?"

"Kegs?" he exclaimed vacantly. "What kegs?"

"The three kegs or ankers, with Glynn's treasure in them."

"You don't mean to say you found the treasure," he cried with a miserable pretence of surprise.

"You know I did," said I; "and you've filched it."

"I assure you, Mr Cobb," he protested, "that I know nothing about it."

Now it is useless to argue with a liar. I tried a new tack.

"Well," I said, "someone has filched it. So there's the whole thing gone. Every stiver. That is, unless I should have happened to take the wrong kegs."

"The wrong kegs!" he gasped. "Why – how could you?"

"Why, you see, that old fool Glynn must needs give you nine ankers to choose from instead of simply hiding the three. I took the three heaviest but I had no time to see what was in them. They may be the wrong ones. I hope they are."

"So do I," said Burbler. And then he was silent and very thoughtful.

"Now listen," I said, after a pause. "I'm going to make you an offer. Will you share the treasure with me wherever it is?"

"I tell you I haven't got it," he replied doggedly; and I washed my hands of him. I had given him a handsome chance and would have been fool enough to stand by my promise. Now he shouldn't have any.

"Will you share with me," I said, "if I tell you where the hiding-place is?"

He shook his head and repeated that "he hadn't got it".

"Think it over," I urged. "I'll just walk on slowly and leave you to consider my offer. Don't refuse offhand. You can overtake me and give me your decision."

With this I strolled on and left him. I knew what he would do, for neither the boat nor the dummies could be far away. But they must have been nearer than I thought, for I had not gone above a half a mile when I heard him running to overtake me and panting heavily. I halted, and as he came up I asked:

"Well? What is your decision?"

"Phoo!" he gasped. "I've – phoo! – thought it over – Mr Cobb – and it seems –ha– only fair to –ha– let you have your half. Don't wanter be greedy."

"Where are the kegs?" I asked.

"In the boat. Boat's in the dyke."

We turned back together and presently Burbler asked:

"Er – where did you say you found the stuff?"

I shook my head. "Wait till we've had a look at the kegs," I replied.

A few minutes more brought us to the dyke, and there was the boat, snugly stowed out of sight under a clump of bush-willows. Burbler hauled it out by the sunken painter and displayed the three kegs – all wet from recent submersion. We both got into the boat and Burbler took the sculls, leaving me to examine the kegs – all of which had been broached and hastily reheaded.

"Before you open them," said Burbler, "tell me where you found them."

"In the cellar," I replied. "Pull out the middle step and you'll find a secret passage. But I'll show you when we get back."

Burbler pulled a few strokes and then awkwardly ran into the bank. He stood up as if to push off, but instead, leaped ashore with both sculls in his hands and, giving the bow of the boat a shove with his foot that sent her out into midstream, threw the sculls away and ran off as hard as he could go towards the inn.

I laughed joyously as he disappeared into the darkness. A few minutes paddling with my open hand brought the boat to the opposite bank, where I landed and towed her down to the tree to which I had secured her before and now again made fast. But I didn't need her after all. For just as I had hauled up my three kegs from the dyke, I heard the sound of wheels on a hidden byroad that crossed the marshes hard by. It turned out to be the rural carrier's cart, returning to Canterbury for the night, with ample accommodation for one passenger and three small kegs. Less than an hour later I sat alone and at peace in a first-class carriage bound for Charing Cross; and on the hat-rack above reposed the "ankores three" with their contents of "goode redd golde".

I live at Elham Manor nowadays, of which house I own the freehold. The Royal George is also my property, subject to Mrs Hodger's tenancy. At the inn resides, as a permanent boarder, a pensioner of mine; a retired police officer, who spends most of his time in the unsuccessful pursuit of the Fordidge trout. His name, by the way, is Burbler.

R Austin Freeman

The D'Arblay Mystery

When a man is found floating beneath the skin of a green-skimmed pond one morning, Dr Thorndyke becomes embroiled in an astonishing case. This wickedly entertaining detective fiction reveals that the victim was murdered through a lethal injection and someone out there is trying a cover-up.

Dr Thorndyke Intervenes

What would you do if you opened a package to find a man's head? What would you do if the headless corpse had been swapped for a case of bullion? What would you do if you knew a brutal murderer was out there, somewhere, and waiting for you? Some people would run. Dr Thorndyke intervenes.

R Austin Freeman

Felo De Se

John Gillam was a gambler. John Gillam faced financial ruin and was the victim of a sinister blackmail attempt. John Gillam is now dead. In this exceptional mystery, Dr Thorndyke is brought in to untangle the secrecy surrounding the death of John Gillam, a man not known for insanity and thoughts of suicide.

Flighty Phyllis

Chronicling the adventures and misadventures of Phyllis Dudley, Richard Austin Freeman brings to life a charming character always getting into scrapes. From impersonating a man to discovering mysterious trap doors, *Flighty Phyllis* is an entertaining glimpse at the times and trials of a wayward woman.

R Austin Freeman

Helen Vardon's Confession

Through the open door of a library, Helen Vardon hears an argument that changes her life forever. Helen's father and a man called Otway argue over missing funds in a trust one night. Otway proposes a marriage between him and Helen in exchange for his co-operation and silence. What transpires is a captivating tale of blackmail, fraud and death. Dr Thorndyke is left to piece together the clues in this enticing mystery.

Mr Pottermack's Oversight

Mr Pottermack is a law-abiding, settled homebody who has nothing to hide until the appearance of the shadowy Lewison, a gambler and blackmailer with an incredible story. It appears that Pottermack is in fact a runaway prisoner, convicted of fraud, and Lewison is about to spill the beans unless he receives a large bribe in return for his silence. But Pottermack protests his innocence, and resolves to shut Lewison up once and for all. Will he do it? And if he does, will he get away with it?

OTHER TITLES BY R AUSTIN FREEMAN AVAILABLE DIRECT FROM HOUSE OF STRATUS

Quantity		£	$(US)	$(CAN)	€
☐	A CERTAIN DR THORNDYKE	6.99	11.50	16.95	11.50
☐	THE D'ARBLAY MYSTERY	6.99	11.50	16.95	11.50
☐	DR THORNDYKE INTERVENES	6.99	11.50	16.95	11.50
☐	DR THORNDYKE'S CASEBOOK	6.99	11.50	16.95	11.50
☐	THE EYE OF OSIRIS	6.99	11.50	16.95	11.50
☐	FELO DE SE	6.99	11.50	16.95	11.50
☐	FLIGHTY PHYLLIS	6.99	11.50	16.95	11.50
☐	THE GOLDEN POOL: A STORY OF A FORGOTTEN MINE	6.99	11.50	16.95	11.50
☐	THE GREAT PORTRAIT MYSTERY	6.99	11.50	16.95	11.50
☐	HELEN VARDON'S CONFESSION	6.99	11.50	16.95	11.50

ALL HOUSE OF STRATUS BOOKS ARE AVAILABLE FROM GOOD BOOKSHOPS OR DIRECT FROM THE PUBLISHER:

Internet: www.houseofstratus.com including author interviews, reviews, features.

Email: sales@houseofstratus.com please quote author, title and credit card details.

OTHER TITLES BY R AUSTIN FREEMAN AVAILABLE DIRECT
FROM HOUSE OF STRATUS

Quantity		£	$(US)	$(CAN)	€
☐	MR POLTON EXPLAINS	6.99	11.50	16.95	11.50
☐	MR POTTERMACK'S OVERSIGHT	6.99	11.50	16.95	11.50
☐	THE MYSTERY OF 31 NEW INN	6.99	11.50	16.95	11.50
☐	THE MYSTERY OF ANGELINA FROOD	6.99	11.50	16.95	11.50
☐	THE PENROSE MYSTERY	6.99	11.50	16.95	11.50
☐	THE PUZZLE LOCK	6.99	11.50	16.95	11.50
☐	THE RED THUMB MARK	6.99	11.50	16.95	11.50
☐	THE SHADOW OF THE WOLF	6.99	11.50	16.95	11.50
☐	A SILENT WITNESS	6.99	11.50	16.95	11.50
☐	THE SINGING BONE	6.99	11.50	16.95	11.50
☐	WHEN ROGUES FALL OUT	6.99	11.50	16.95	11.50

ALL HOUSE OF STRATUS BOOKS ARE AVAILABLE FROM GOOD BOOKSHOPS
OR DIRECT FROM THE PUBLISHER:

Hotline: UK ONLY: 0800 169 1780, please quote author, title and credit card details.
INTERNATIONAL: +44 (0) 20 7494 6400, please quote author, title, and credit card details.

Send to: House of Stratus Sales Department
24c Old Burlington Street
London
W1X 1RL
UK

Please allow for postage costs charged per order plus an amount per book as set out in the tables below:

	£(Sterling)	$(US)	$(CAN)	€(Euros)
Cost per order				
UK	2.00	3.00	4.50	3.30
Europe	3.00	4.50	6.75	5.00
North America	3.00	4.50	6.75	5.00
Rest of World	3.00	4.50	6.75	5.00
Additional cost per book				
UK	0.50	0.75	1.15	0.85
Europe	1.00	1.50	2.30	1.70
North America	2.00	3.00	4.60	3.40
Rest of World	2.50	3.75	5.75	4.25

PLEASE SEND CHEQUE, POSTAL ORDER (STERLING ONLY), EUROCHEQUE, OR INTERNATIONAL MONEY ORDER (PLEASE CIRCLE METHOD OF PAYMENT YOU WISH TO USE)
MAKE PAYABLE TO: STRATUS HOLDINGS plc

Cost of book(s): —————————— Example: 3 x books at £6.99 each: £20.97

Cost of order: —————————— Example: £2.00 (Delivery to UK address)

Additional cost per book: ————— Example: 3 x £0.50: £1.50

Order total including postage: ——— Example: £24.47

Please tick currency you wish to use and add total amount of order:

☐ £ (Sterling)   ☐ $ (US)   ☐ $ (CAN)   ☐ € (EUROS)

VISA, MASTERCARD, SWITCH, AMEX, SOLO, JCB:

☐☐☐☐☐☐☐☐☐☐☐☐☐☐☐☐☐☐☐☐☐☐

Issue number (Switch only):

☐☐☐

Start Date: Expiry Date:

☐☐ / ☐☐   ☐☐ / ☐☐

Signature: _____

NAME: _____

ADDRESS: _____

_____

POSTCODE: _____

Please allow 28 days for delivery.

Prices subject to change without notice.
Please tick box if you do not wish to receive any additional information. ☐

House of Stratus publishes many other titles in this genre; please check our website (**www.houseofstratus.com**) for more details.